THE WATER QUEEN

The Elementals Book 4

Jennifer L. Kelly

Library of Congress PCN: 2017908241

BoxerBull Books

Cleveland, OH

ISBN-10: 0-9977764-7-1
ISBN-13: 978-0-9977764-7-8

TO MY ARC READERS, WHO'VE JOINED ME FOR THE LONG HAUL. MAY YOU COME INTO YOUR OWN POWER. CHOOSE WISELY.
-J.L.K.

OTHER BOOKS BY JENNIFER L. KELLY

THE ELEMENTALS

ARMY OF FIRE
THE EARTH KEY
GENESIS OF WOOD

THE LUCIA CHRONICLES

THE PROPHECY
THE DISSENTIENT
THE BEACON
THE GIRL WHO WASN'T LOVED (NOVELLA)

STAND ALONE FICTION

THE FRACTURED LIFE OF JENNY MCCLAIN

PROLOGUE

I am afraid.

I have a mission.

I am not prepared. But I have no choice.

I am the Impossible Girl. A myth, a legend, a story told to Xon 9 children before they go to sleep at night. A bed time story. Only I'm not. I am very, very real. I didn't ask for this. I didn't ask people to take risks for me. I didn't ask—never would ask—people to *die* for me.

But they do.

And they will continue to do so. Because truthfully, it isn't for me. And it doesn't matter if I asked for it.

Long ago a girl was born to an immortal woman who fell in love with a mortal man. The girl was bequeathed with many gifts from her mother's immortal sisters: The Elemental Goddesses.

Passion like the flickering flames of a roaring fire.

Compassion like the fertile soil giving birth to the most delicate of flowers.

Wisdom like the oldest of trees that have silently watched the passage of centuries.

Intuition like the bottomless depths of the vast sea.

And—

Strength like the strongest of metals.

These were the gifts given to the girl and these were the gifts that the Imminent Darkness wanted to take away. The Universe needed balance and this girl was an anomaly. Mortals and Immortals don't fall in love. She shouldn't exist. But they did. And I do.

In order to protect me, my mother traveled to the mountains of our home planet and to a mystical place called the Elemental Abyss. There she threw in five stones—one for each of Xon 9's Elements: Fire, Earth, Wood, Water, and Metal. With each stone went a piece of my personality, thus fracturing it, so that there was very little semblance of the true Ka Waylon left. Good-bye courage. Good-bye intuition. And forget wisdom. Buh-bye. Except the day came that I had to choose. Which Element did I want to be affiliated with for the rest of my life? I chose Fire. Big mistake.

Soon the truth began to emerge, secrets that had been kept from me for the eighteen years of my life and that could only begin to be revealed on the hundredth solar alignment. Secrets that involved my true identity—the missing parts of who I am—oh, and the whole half-immortal thing. (Very cool.)

Turns out I represent all the possibilities of Xon 9's people. The Imminent Darkness has spent hundreds of years trying to divide us, separating us by our differences. But no more. We no longer need to choose. We are not only passionate like Fire or merely wise like Wood. We are everything: strong like Metal, intuitive like Water, and compassionate like Earth. We can be all of these things. So I say to the Imminent Darkness (because I know that you're listening, you're always listening, behind every whisper or shadow you are waiting): No more.

So you see, I am afraid. I am afraid I will somehow mess up the entire future of my planet. I am afraid that the Imminent Darkness will win. And I am afraid that the most difficult tasks still lay before me.

Luckily, I am not the only one afraid.

Because the Imminent Darkness is afraid of me too.

CHAPTER 1

The coolness of the sea laps at my ankles. I toss a small pebble into the cerulean blue water and listen for the satisfying *plop*! as it breaks the stillness of the surface. Birds chirp in the distance and a soft breeze rustles the shorn hair at the back of my neck, tickling the Elemental Star tattoo that marks my skin. I run my fingers over it, feeling the green vines of Earth that have sprung to life at the tip of the star, and then moving my fingers to the smoothness of the filigree that makes Fire, before lastly running my fingers over my newest addition: the rough ridges of bark. Wood. Three stones retrieved. My fingers find the flat smoothness that is Metal and Water, the two stones I have yet to retrieve. Because those Elements have not been returned to me, those portions of my Elemental Star remain dormant, just regular inked skin.

I close my eyes, allowing the colors of the sunset to dance across my eyelids. This is Earth. Well, not really. Not even Old Earth if we're being technical. But Earth as my mother imagines it. A Land created by Raj and Katayun, the Father and Mother of the entire Universe, to placate their feuding daughters. Five sisters. Five goddesses. Five lands. Five elements. Simple math. I was never much good at math though.

Someone sits beside me. I feel the ever-so-slight shift in the pink sand beneath me. I've been heightened. I can feel—and see—things that I've never felt or seen in my entire life. The smell of soap, leather, and salty sea drift over to me and I smile. I open my eyes and Sloan puts an arm around my waist, scooting me closer to him. Sloan is my boyfriend. He was my teacher, but before you get all weird about it, he is only four years older than me, making him twenty-two. On Xon 9 we only attend two years of University. Well, that's how it used to be before the whole operation got shut down. Thanks or no thanks to me.

Sloan is my protector, quite literally. He took an oath many years ago when his mother, Bina, had a vision of the Impossible Girl arriving on Xon 9. In order to fulfill his oath he took a teaching position until I came along. And that's when things changed. A lot. At first I thought it was creepy how he was always watching me and encouraging me to stand up for myself. Actually, I realize now he was encouraging me to be myself. Period. Only I didn't understand at the time. Now, I know better. Poor guy, not only took an Everlasting Vow, he even went and fell in love with the very girl he was meant to protect. Luckily for me.

I take in his shaggy brown hair that is in sore need of a cutting. It hangs into his brilliant green eyes, which are framed by long dark lashes. The right side of his face is lined with silvery-green scales that fade away into the collar of his black t-shirt. Gills mark either side of his neck, which is convenient since he's a Water. Funny, that he represents the very thing I am afraid of most. Besides the Imminent Darkness.

"I don't want to leave." I rest my head on his shoulder.

"I know." He tilts my cheek so that we're face to face and kisses me gently as if I was some fragile, breakable thing. Which we both know I am not. I am not only each of my Elements that has been returned to me, but I am each of my Elements at an exponential level. I guess that's what happens when a group of Immortals get in on the gift-giving. Go big or go home.

He pulls away carefully, but our hipbones are still pressed against one another. The sea laps softly in front of us. Who would want to leave this? He turns so that the smooth, angular side of his face is in my direction and stares at the sea. I know he loves it too. This place—unlike the red barrenness of Xon 9—is a bountiful world of color, sound, and mystery. But it won't be long before the Imminent Darkness returns here. It tried once. And it will try again. One by one, the ID seems to ruin everything that I've come to love. Or that I try to love.

The sun eases itself down past the horizon leaving a line of golden-white light across the sky, caressing against the indigo of the night. Tiny pinpricks of light begin popping out across the vastness above our heads, billions of stars seeming to blink on, come to bid us good-night. You'd think it was impossible there could be so many stars. But you may have figured out how I feel about impossible things.

"We should go." And I know he means that we should return to the castle, where my mother and father are, and where Ahna and Li are waiting for us. I nod and Sloan helps me to my feet, pulling me up from the sand, which now coats the seat of my shorts and the backs of my legs. When he pulls me up, he doesn't let go. "You don't have to do this," he whispers.

I sigh. "You know that I do."

"No. I want to be clear. You get a choice in this, Ka. No matter what anyone else says or wants you to do. It's your choice. It always has been."

"What choice is there when there isn't one?"

"Not doing is a choice too."

I turn into his arms so that my forehead is even with his chin. "That's the coward's way."

"Your Metal hasn't been restored yet," he says, referring to the Element that is both the strongest and most feared of Xon 9. Not to mention the most misunderstood. And I can feel him smile from the movement of his chin. "Or is there something you want to tell me?"

"Trust me. No Metal yet. I'd think if I had it, I wouldn't feel so afraid."

"Maybe. But fear is good. I know plenty of Metals who

16

experience fear. Luckily, fear can help keep us from making irrational decisions, if we acknowledge it. Being afraid and still being willing to go forward, that right there is called courage."

I pull back slightly so that I can see his eyes. The Land of Earth's single moon reflects a sliver of light in the green pools that gaze down at me.

"You think I'm courageous?"

He grins. "More than anyone I know." He kisses my forehead then takes my hand leading me away from the beach and back toward the castle, which from here looms large and pristine above us, golden warmth emitting from its windows, beckoning us back. "And Ka, I think you've made your choice quite clear."

I intertwine my fingers with his, a tether that always reminds me of who I am and what matters most. "I don't follow."

"Fear is a choice too."

. . .

I never used to be afraid. Not like this. But I've seen things and once you've seen things, you can't unsee them. The Imminent Darkness is as old as the Universe itself, the same Universe that birthed my mother, the Immortal Earth Goddess with three faces: Anuja, Novea, and Kesara. The ID is all about power and uses the fear that it creates to manipulate people and bend them to its will. It is ancient and formless, feeding on the negative energy of the devastation left in its wake, which only makes it grow stronger. And its appetite is ravenous because with each retrieval of a stone, I grow stronger and the Imminent Darkness becomes weaker. My mom said it's all about balance. Unfortunately, I'm what is causing the imbalance.

The castle appears stark on the outside with its white stone walls, but what it lacks in ambience on the outside, it makes up for on the inside. In the backyard is a lush garden with a pergola and a long table for outdoor dinners. It rarely rains here—only for short periods of time to keep everything thriving—after all, this is my mother's world. Inside the main doors is a purple runner atop the polished, white stone floor that leads to a wooden throne upholstered in amethyst-colored velvet. There are many nooks and crannies in the castle, including a winding staircase with an elaborate banister that leads to six spacious bedrooms and six bathrooms. Why anyone would ever need six bathrooms is beyond me, especially since our family only consists of me, Mom, and Dad, but I suspect it has something to do with Mom holding out the hope that she and her sisters can someday reconcile.

I have four aunts: Celosia, Isa, Constancia, and Tullia. The rulers of the lands of Fire, Metal, Wood, and Water respectively. I've only met the two and let's just say I could see maybe why Celosia and Mom didn't get along. The Land of Fire is all fire and brimstone, quite literally. My aunt Constancia I've only met in avian form, but she was very kind as far as birds go. Many moons ago, my mom and her sisters were each given their own land after a codger tricked them. He gave them each a stone and the sisters fought over whose stone was more special, until Raj and Katayun could no longer bear it and created a land for each of their daughters to rule over. Separately.

The codger, of course, was the Imminent Darkness looking to divide the sisters who had once loved one another so dearly, in order to cause chaos. Like Mom said, balance and all that junk. And yet, despite everything, my aunts were overjoyed with my birth, much to the ID's disappointment. They gifted me the very stones that were later used to protect me, and which I am now retrieving. If that's not a peace offering, I'm not sure what is.

We make our way to the living area with its large stone fireplace with wood mantle, decorated in pictures of yours truly. Above it is an oil painting of a brilliant cyan-colored dragonfly, a homage to another one of my mother's many forms. Two walls are lined floor-to-ceiling with books and the third wall, across from the entrance, is a set of glass doors that lead out to the garden. My father has started a fire and he sits on one of the soft purple couches beside my mother. Both of them are reading. Ahna sits in the plush violet armchair and she too is engrossed in a book about as thick as a tree trunk. The only one not reading is Ahna's twin brother, Li, who is sprawled across the remaining couch, his lanky form taking up all three cushions in their entirety.

I feel a pang of guilt at Li's presence. His too long black hair that falls carelessly into his almond-shaped eyes, the wide nose, and perfectly arched lips. Perfect, if not for the black tribal-looking tattoo that now runs down the right side of his face, curling down his neck and into the collar of his t-shirt. Li and I were never a *thing* exactly. I've known him forever and he's one of my best friends, but he was my first kiss. And the only kiss I'd ever experienced before Sloan. Li was the forbidden fruit, taking me to the Black Bazaar and making me feel things I probably shouldn't be feeling. But he's always been there for me, even when he was unwillingly turned into a soldier to be used against me—against the Leadership Council of Xon 9—in the name of the Imminent Darkness. And yet, his love for me was strong enough to break the bonds of collective consciousness, if even for the briefest of moments, to warn me. That kind of loyalty and that kind of love is what makes my stomach now twist up in a knot. *We are not the same people.* I remind myself of his words. We've both changed. And Li doesn't even know the half of it.

Not only did he lose his Fire because of my actions, but the Imminent Darkness took his form in order to attack me, using Li as if he were nothing more than a pawn in some sort of sick game. It almost—I almost—killed him for a second time, but luckily was quick thinking enough to use my ring to bring us here. My ring was made by my friend Doran using the turquoise pieces of the destroyed Earth stone. It has a living memory which can return me home whenever I want it. Or need it. My mother used the nectar of the Wood stone to save Li and now, you'd never know he was on the brink of death only several days ago. The part that he doesn't know is my mother happened to make him immortal in the process. Not just half-immortal like me, but full-on totally immortal. That kind of thing would just go straight to his head.

Li looks up at the sound of our arrival. "Hey, Kata," he says and winks at me. Like I said straight to his head. He's fiddling with something in his hands, but I can't tell what it is.

"You take up the entire couch like you own the place. Move over," I order. He obliges, sitting up and moving over to make enough room for both Sloan and myself. I can see now that the object is some kind of wooden puzzle cube with sliding pieces. Each piece a different color. It must belong to my mom. She loves puzzles and riddles. "A little primitive for your tastes, isn't it?"

Li scoffs. "Actually, I'm finding it quite challenging. You see I have to align each piece so an entire side of the cube is all the same color."

Mother closes her book. "Your father made that for me. It's modeled after some Old Earth toy." She smiles warmly at Dad, who is oblivious, still engrossed in his own book.

"Here, let me see it." Ahna reaches across the space between the chair and sofa, snatching the cube from Li. She flips her thick braid over her shoulder and bites her bottom lip as she slides and moves about the pieces. In a matter of minutes she's solved the puzzle, each side now made up of a single color.

"Well done!" Mom claps which finally causes Dad to look up. My father is a Wood and was a liege to the Council before he came to the Land of Earth. The Leadership Council is the governing body of Xon 9 and is made up of five Woods, four males and one female. Wood is considered unyielding and steadfast. They have a reputation for making the best leaders. The lines between Council and Imminent Darkness are too blurred for my taste, as the Imminent Darkness has its share of followers on Xon 9. Only, they're none the wiser to the fact that the ID is using them to feed, not the other way around, and in the process breeding aggression and paranoia, in corruption with its negative energy.

Li scowls. "You take the fun out of everything."

I feel Sloan laugh silently beside me. Ahna was always an excellent student, especially in Earth Science and Universal History, her two favorite subjects.

"So," my father says setting his book on the arm of the couch, "are you kids ready to return home?"

Ahna nods anxiously. "Yes. I'm worried about Mom and Dad." Mr. and Mrs. Solloman, Li, and Ahna, were our neighbors. Now our house sits vacant next to theirs. There's no reason for us to go back. But Li and Ahna need to go back.

"I'm sure they're fine. They're no fun just like you," Li says.

Ahna sticks her tongue out. "Well, some of us follow the rules so we don't get ourselves into trouble like you." Li definitely is the black sheep of the Solloman family. He's all fiery passion and impulsivity. Or at least he was. For a long time after the army of Fire incident, he didn't seem like himself. This back and forth banter reminds me of the old Li.

"I agree with Li," I say. "I'm sure they're fine, Ahna. Your Mom and Dad obey all the rules and don't draw attention to themselves. If anything, they're probably just worried sick about you guys." There was no way of telling Mr. and Mrs. Solloman what happened or where we went when we left Xon 9. The Imminent Darkness's presence was growing stronger, curfews were being implemented, among other rules to try and keep the colonists safe…or out of the way. If we tried to contact them, the Imminent Darkness could have followed us. Or worse, tried to hurt Mr. or Mrs. Solloman.

Ahna's brown eyes fall on me. They used to be warm and inviting, sometimes chastising at my procrastinating ways in school, but now there's something different there that looks back at me. A bit of iciness mixed with wariness. I almost killed her twin. I can understand the chill beneath her gaze, but surely she knows I love Li as much as she does. Right?

"Yes, I suppose so." Her tone is clipped, but then she shakes her head and smiles as if willing herself to not let that small sliver of hatred show. "Tomorrow then?"

"I think it would be best," my mother agrees.

"Ka and I think it's time we go too," Sloan says looking at me sideways.

"Yeah, I don't think I can put it off any longer. The longer I wait, the more damage the Imminent Darkness is doing." I glance at Li who is still scowling down at the solved puzzle in his hands. "And now that Li's better, I guess we don't have a reason to continue to stay."

"Don't be silly. This is your home," Mom says, but her gray eyes betray her worry.

"Kata's right," Dad says. "There are two stones left and each moment she isn't looking for them, is a moment the Imminent Darkness grows stronger. Tomorrow, Sloan and Ka can head to Tullia's Land, and I'll take Li and Ahna back to the colony."

The only thing is now that the ID has infiltrated the Elemental

Abyss, where the portals to the five lands are located, and destroyed the magical creatures that protect it, I'm not sure how we're going anywhere.

Mom shakes her head. "Are you sure that's a good idea Absalom?"

"I'll pop in and out and be back before you're even up for breakfast." Dad grins.

"You'll be taking the watch then?"

Dad holds up his wrist and taps the sapphire watch face. "You bet."

Li looks up. "That looks like an ordinary watch to me." Li wasn't conscious when we used my ring to come here.

"It has a living memory." I hold up my index finger. "Like my ring. It can return to the last place that it was or, in my case, Mom made it so I can come home when I need to. It's how we brought you here."

"Huh. That's crazy." Li shakes his head in disbelief then glances up, a sly smile spreading across his angular face. And I know exactly what he's thinking before he even says it. Because this is the Li I know. The lover of cloaking cuffs and pleasure patches. Mischievous. Entrepreneurial. And a little bit brazen. "I bet there's a huge market for something like that back home. Because you know, I happen to know a guy."

Chapter 2

That night I can't sleep. I lay awake staring at the ceiling. My room at the castle is empty of my presence. It is a temporary place. Somewhere that I can rest my head in between jumping from Land to Land in search of the stones. It doesn't feel like home. Then again. Home no longer feels like home either.

Instead of the soft pink light filtering through my bedroom window, crisp white light shines through the open window. A cool breeze rustles the white lacey curtains. The walls in this room are a soft lilac. My mother obviously has a thing for purple, which also explains my purple room back home. I just never felt a need to change it. And now I see why she may have chosen that color. Purple is the color of royalty. Am I royalty? I don't feel like it.

I grew up on Xon 9. Hundreds of years ago, Old Earth scientists realized the sun was going to die. Makes sense because we knew that the sun was a star and eventually everything has to die (in one way or another). So they sent out probes into the Universe and found Xon 9 with its barren red landscape, strange silvery-green foliage, red sun and twin moons. Oh, and the most important thing. Xon 9 had water, not surface water, but water just below the surface which could easily be extracted. And so 3,000 people from Old Earth were selected to start a colony on Xon 9. That was a long time ago, and the population hasn't grown very much since then. Maybe it's because people are too busy to worry about getting busy, or maybe it's because of something more sinister. Hard to say.

Some people—like Sloan's mother, Bina—think that the Imminent Darkness has prevented our progress. I can't argue because I kind of agree. It makes sense. We have access to advanced technology, like Li and his cloaking cuffs and teleportation portals that have all but been banned, and yet we live fairly primitively in concrete, wood, or stone houses. Some buildings are made of sleek glass and metal, like where Sloan's sister Michaela lives, in the military complex. Some of these dwelling choices are prone to Elemental affiliation. Has our existence on Xon 9 somehow thrown out the balance of the Universe?

One thing the Old Earth scientists and astrophysicists didn't bargain for was the strong elements of their new home. The planet had a unique physiological effect on its habitants. But it didn't take long before they learned how to control the elements. They realized the elements began to most influence our biology around the middle to end of puberty, so during our last year of school, everyone had to Pronounce an Elemental. Once, you join your fellow Elementals, you participate in a ceremony that begins the Transitional Phase, along with an injection that helps expedite the Change. Sometimes, like with Li and Ahna, you can feel a particular Element calling to you. It didn't surprise me that Li Pronounced Fire or that Ahna Pronounced Earth, but what did surprise everyone was when I Pronounced Fire. Because I was anything but fiery to say the least.

I close my eyes thinking back to the Black Box at Pronouncement. Once inside it would scan your body, stating certain personality traits, then give a recommendation as to which Elemental to choose. Then it was up to you. Five buttons, glowing silently, waited for the press of your fingertips. My friend Doran grew up a Metal in the Underground. And he is a Metal through and through: strong, witty, determined…and a little rebellious. But he chose Fire because he knew what could happen when a Metal became Unbalanced. When any Element became Unbalanced. Like his father.

My mind drifts to Doran and his sister Zora, the tattooist who gave me my Elemental Star. I've no idea where they are and I'm worried about them. The Imminent Darkness has claimed the Underground causing them to flee. I can only hope that they, along with their Mother—a compassionate and wise woman who is all soft edges and warm hugs—are somewhere safe.

I don't know much about Doran's father. He was a Water. I know he somehow became Unbalanced, but that's all I know. The bits and pieces I have are memories that slipped from Doran's consciousness into my consciousness traveling through the portal from the Land of Fire. He didn't tell me. And I didn't ask.

The Black Box recommended I choose Water. Of course, you don't have to listen to the Black Box's recommendation. Of course, I didn't listen to the Black Box's recommendation. Of course, I chose Fire. And, well, that didn't turn out as well as I'd hoped. And now it doesn't even matter. The choosing. Pronouncement. It means nothing now. The University Complex is closed indefinitely, the Elemental leaders of the various New Elemental Program being interrogated for signs of possible corruption. What once seemed the most important choice of my entire life, reduced to something child-like and silly. Why choose when truthfully there is no choice? Do we not each have a little bit of each Element within us all? I've seen it myself. No one is all one or the other. Least of all, myself.

I am all possibilities. I am all of the Elements, just as it should be. For all of us. I have the boldness of Metal and the reliability of Wood. I can be soft and nurturing like Earth, or passionate and angry like Fire. Sometimes I am fluid and gentle like Water. I am not only this or only that. I am all of these things and more. And yet.

I am afraid. The thought of traveling to the Land of Water makes my stomach gnarl with anxiety. At first I thought it was because I don't really know how to swim, not having surface water on Xon 9 didn't lend itself to many opportunities to learn, but Sloan has taught me the basics in preparation for our trip. Still. There's something there gnawing at the edges, and where I once was boldly (almost recklessly) unafraid, I now have the heavy weight of fear that's taken up residence in my chest. I've always known that Water is different than any of the other Elements, and Sloan is always quick to remind me. Water gives us life, but in the next crash and fall of the wave it can take that same life away. Water is nurturing, serene, and compassionate. But it is also destructive and temperamental.

And that's what scares me. We all have parts of our personality we'd rather not show. The ugly parts. The dark parts. It isn't always sunshine and unicorns. There's that word again: *Balance*. No, it isn't so much the Water itself that makes me afraid, but more so what it will mean once my Water is restored back to me.

Once I have it returned, who is it that I will become?

. . .

I don't know where I am. Well, let me correct myself. I know that I am laying in my bed in my room in the castle, and yet at the same time I am very aware that I am not there. At least not consciously. I know what this means and it is only a matter of time before someone shows up. I take a moment to look at my surroundings.

It's dark out. The sky is a clear midnight. Billions of stars paint across the night sky. A round, white moon hangs above. Beneath my bare feet is a rocky shore and before me is more sky. Wait. Wrong. Not sky. *Sea*. Dark water mirrors back the reflection of the sky. I involuntarily shudder. As hard as I've tried to learn to love the water it still frightens me. Sure, I can swim now, even dance with the water as if we are intimate partners, and yet the unpredictability of its nature and the mystery of its fathomless depths makes me uneasy.

The rocks beneath my feet glow white in the moonlight and feel smooth. Perhaps sometimes the water surges and covers this shoreline. Sloan has mentioned something about tides and the moon, but it's lost on me not having the Water education he has had. Not to mention Xon 9 has no surface water. No one comes. There's no bobbing head of shaggy, chestnut brown hair swimming toward me. My mother doesn't magically appear on the beach—if you could call it that—beside me. The people in my life having many gifts and talents. Some are natural like Doran's ability to craft beautiful jewelry out of junk metal, and others are supernatural like Sloan's ability to read my mind. Which he swears he's been trying not to do. We had a slightly heated argument about the violation of privacy when he slips into my mind. A girl's got to have some secrets, something for herself to make her smile or to make her cry, to show that she's still human. That she's real. Oh, and then there's the dream walking. And I'm pretty sure that's what's happening. Just no one has shown up yet. I may be the Impossible Girl, but in a lot of ways I'm still pretty ordinary. No dream-walking or animorphis here, and only a little bit of future-seeing thanks to my new Wood superpower.

The near silence is eerie. Just the soft lapping of the water against the rocks. I hate to turn my back on the unknown vastness before me, but at the same time the curiosity of what's behind me is killing me. So I turn around careful not to slip on the smooth rocks. Behind me is a dark forest, but I can see between the black trees and the slivers of night sky in between them. I look over my right shoulder. No one in the water. Perhaps my visitor is waiting for me somewhere else. I decide it can't hurt to explore. I'm sure if I was in any danger I could just wake myself up. My skin prickles and I wish that I slept in something more than a tank top and shorts.

My feet make no sound as I make my way across the stones. I stick my arms out for a little bit of balance, but it isn't long before the stones give way to smaller stones and eventually to dirt. I scan the forest for a path of some kind and at first I don't see one, but then on my second scan I notice it. It's overgrown with long, blades of seagrass. I make my way toward it. No birds are chirping, no squirrels or other animals chittering. Just complete silence like a heavy cloak that's wrapped around my shoulders. The forest quickly ends, opening up on another shoreline. The dark sea greeting me once again. I realize I'm on an island.

However, this side is slightly different than the other. Instead of stones, the grass and dirt mix with a soft sand that looks luminescent in the light of the moon. To my right the shoreline curves back the way I came and to my left is a small structure. It almost looks like one of the castle's turrets, except it isn't attached to any other building, just a tower-like structure standing cock-eyed on the beach. I approach the tower and notice green vines growing along its side, and I can't help but wonder if someone once lived here. My dreams aren't always my dreams. Sometimes I end up in places that someone else has conjured and seemingly planted into my consciousness, either to deliver a message, or a warning.

As I near the turret, I can see a soft, warm glow coming from within. Like the flicker of a candle or lantern. Someone's home. There doesn't seem to be a proper door, but there's a slim window—

and I use that term loosely—that's about ground-level. I use my hands to hoist myself up, careful not to scrape my knees on the rough stone. Once, I'm inside the light source casts odd shadows on the otherwise empty space. I step through an arched doorway and follow the golden glow up a narrow flight of stairs, so snug that I have to duck to avoid hitting my head. The staircase winds gently and I find myself on the second level.

In front of me hangs a tapestry. It has a star on it that very much resembles the one on the back of my neck. I reach out to touch it. The fabric is velvety soft and luxurious between my fingers. To my left the stairwell opens onto a large a room. A single lantern sits on a table, glowing like a beacon. The furnishings are sparse. Besides the table and the lantern, there is a wooden chair. That's it. As I move into the room to get a closer look, I realize there's a book on the table. And that it's open. I almost wish I was having a dream visitation from Sloan or my mother. Even from Bina. This—whatever this is—is quite unexpected. I shiver as I remember the dreams where the Imminent Darkness paid me a visit. But somehow this feels different.

I pull the chair away from the desk, behind me is another window and the moonlight pours in, its beam falling across the open book. I look around once more, half expecting someone to manifest, but no one does. Resigned to the fact that this is a solo visit, I sit down in the chair and scoot it in closer to the desk. It scrapes across the stone and the sound seems garish in the stillness. I glance again at the tapestry with my Elemental Star shimmering with its fancy golden, emerald, sapphire, bronze, and silver threads. It looks like something appropriate for a castle. For royalty. Where is it that I am?

The book is open and written in a language that I cannot identify. The pages are old and yellowed. I rest my arm across the pages to mark the space, and flip the book to see the cover. Supple brown leather and no title. Not very helpful. I lay the cover back down and take in the pages that were left waiting for me. Even if no one is here to visit me, I know that there is always a message to discover. Or something to learn. I just have to find it. My eyes scan the text. I notice a black smudge in a margin. This text was hand-written. But by who? I continue to scan and go to turn the page, when it slices my finger tip. A papercut. Stupid. Only I would get a papercut in a dream. A small droplet of blood, round with possibility drops onto the page of the book.

I stick my index finger in my mouth and turn the page. I don't know what I'm looking for, a picture maybe to help me figure out the meaning of the text. But as I continue to scan the next page, something strange happens. The words on the page seem to swirl and coalesce. I blink once. Twice. Three times. Still moving. Moving. As if they were alive. Blood. Is it possible my blood brought these words to life? Finally, the words seem to be pleased with their new locations and the text settles down once again. Only this time I can read what it says. And it's about me.

CHAPTER 3

This isn't the legend of the Impossible Girl. This is truly about me. My life as I know it, not some made up fairy tale. Or Seer's prediction. Not that I discount Bina or Raj and Katayun for that matter. I flip through the pages. Any coldness I felt has disappeared, my heart thumping in my chest as I read.

There's the time that my mother sought out the help of Bina when as a child I showed aptitude for all of the Elements. There's a bit about Sloan and his Everlasting Vow and the villainous Diadona, a perfectly coifed bully who picked on me for no reason other than I was me. And then there's me and Li, staring dreamily at each other beneath a lamp post in the Black Bazaar before he puts his lips on mine and I find myself kissing him back for the first time.

The story fast forwards to the Ritual of Fire and then to the army of Fire where I witness Everly evaporate and Li's body barely breathing. It seems that I can't turn the pages fast enough. There I am finding my mother on the floor of her study, bleeding, almost dead before we use the Earth key to travel to safety. The mummy—the Imminent Darkness—in the mysterious pyramid. Tristen, half-woman and half-snake before the Earth stone kills her. I slow down as I come to the parts about the Land of Wood and the Fairy Grove, a pang in my heart at the mention of Qildor's name. Qildor, the Keeper of the Genesis, a valiant warrior, and a loyal friend. When I get to the part where the Imminent Darkness takes over Li's body and attacks me. I slam it shut. The rest of the pages contain more. But I don't want to know.

I get up and pace the diameter of the small room. The flame of the lantern flickers as if it too is a part of me, following me back and forth. I pause. I squat and the flame shrinks. I jump up as high as I can reach and the flame leaps at the same time. I move left and the flame follows. I move right and it follows me once more. I am connected to the flame. Turning my back on it, I lean my elbows on the ledge of the window and look out at the sea lit up by the moonlight. What is this place? Why was I brought here? If it was to see my future, then this place better rethink its purpose, because that is not something I want to see.

"Are yeh sure about that?" A familiar voice says from behind me.

I turn to find Bina sitting in a wooden rocking chair that seems grossly out of place in the sparse turret. She looks mostly as she always does: frizzy gray hair in a halo around her head, pale gray eyes, tanned, wrinkled skin. Her mouth forms a straight line except for the corners, which are upturned slightly. Her life has not worn her well and she looks like she could be Sloan's grandmother instead of his mother. She's wearing a multicolored crocheted shawl over her shoulders and what appears to be some sort of plain, sack-like dress. Her feet are bare. The bare light of the room bounces off the metallic threads that line the side of her face. Sloan may be a Water, but the rest of his family are Metals. A choice that I don't think was necessarily his first, but that he felt had to be made. In order for some girl he didn't even yet know, to later trust him with her life.

"You know I hate when you do that." She smiles in acknowledgement. This is where Sloan gets his many talents from. "What it this place?" I take the chair and move it so that I'm sitting on the other side of the table, across from Bina. She rocks gently back and forth before answering.

"A sanctuary."

"Whose?" I ask even though I already know.

"Yers."

"Why?"

She takes some time to answer, the silence stretching across like a bridge between us, two people asleep in different worlds, but very much awake in this dream one. I know that I will wake up with complete memory of this conversation. In the past I have even awoken with a memento beneath my pillow. Sloan once explained it to me, that dream walking is actually fairly easy because it's simply another plane of existence. And once you learn how to send your mind from one plane to another, the more you do it, it becomes almost as natural as breathing. Dreams aren't your subconscious, he told me as we sat on the beach well into the morning hours, they're another existence altogether. *Like the portals in the Elemental Abyss?* I had asked. *Exactly, like that,* he had replied.

Finally, when I think she may have fallen asleep, Bina speaks. "Because, as I think yeh are already aware, things are about to get more difficult." She pauses waiting for a reaction, but I only nod. "And there may come a time when yeh need to seek refuge. This—" she gestures at the room "—is where you will go."

Bina can be very vague at times, but I press her anyways. "And why exactly will I need refuge?"

She smiles one of her toothless smiles. "Water is very powerful."

"It gives life, but it can take life away," I say. "Sloan's reminded me many times."

"It is not something that ye should forget."

I gesture behind me. "What's with the room? And the freaky lantern?"

"Well, as I said, it's yer room. But this room is very old. This island is very old. Much older than yeh. I suppose ye could say it had been waiting for yeh." She takes up rocking back and forth, the chair making a muffled squeaking sound on the backward motion. I realize she isn't going to elaborate, so I decide to move on. I'm not sure how dream time works, but I feel that I've been here for hours and before I know it, the Land of Earth's brilliant golden sun will be shining through my window.

"You said things were about to get difficult. Haven't they been difficult already?" I think about the book and the images of Li that I can't shake from my mind, despite his relaxed banter and his as-yet-to-be-discovered immortality. Immortality doesn't necessarily mean invincible. The thought of losing him a third time makes my heart clench in my chest.

"The Land of Water is an interesting place."

"They've all been an interesting place." I point out. "Except maybe the Land of Fire. That one was just downright terrifying." An image of the erupting volcano and Doran's hand in mine comes floating back to me. And I wonder...

"He is safe. Zora too." She nods, completing my thought for me. "Ye must remember, Kata, that Sloan is a Water." It's so rare that Bina uses my name, that my interest in the conversation has become more piqued. Also, she didn't just call me Ka, she called me Kata, which is a nickname only those close to me know about. Ka, my birth name, means Fire, the one Element that I probably lacked the most. But Kata, after my immortal grandmother, Katayun, means *pure one*. There are no coincidences with Bina. Every gesture, every word, has a purpose.

"Yes. He's been...he's taught me how to swim."

"Ye will need to know more than how to swim in the Land of Water, my girl." She points a bony finger at the book. After the failed MindCleanse, she's seemed even older and more fragile, almost like a shadow of the person she used to be, the woman I visited for a reading one fateful night in the Black Bazaar. A night that, little did I know, would change my life forever. I glance over my shoulder and the book has somehow reopened itself, even though I know that I closed it just a few minutes ago. "The book will help yeh to understand."

I shake my head. "I don't want to know the future."

"Even if you could change it?" She leans forward in the rocker and I fear she may tumble out.

I hesitate to answer. Do I want to know the future? Would I work to change it if I knew? Finally, I answer honestly. "I don't know."

She shakes her head as if I'm being petulant. "Even if it means that you could save the one you love?" The last time Bina said something similar to me it ended up being a metaphor: *When the one you love is lost, the stone will turn to dust.* I feared it could be Sloan or Li, but turns out it was me. The old Ka had to die so the new Ka could come forth. The Ka I used to be washed away, so the Ka I am becoming could emerge. She stares at me intently and I notice how clear her eyes are. When she is seeing the future, sometimes her eyes go white, similar to the blind eyes of Sloan's father, Finn. Finn has no sight—something else the Imminent Darkness robbed him of—and Bina has more sight than any normal person could know what to do with.

I swallow and the noise is audible in the silence that surrounds us. It's as if the entire night has gone still. "Sloan?"

She nods. "Normally, I would not intervene, but..." Her voice trails off and I know Sloan is all she has left. Finn has been wrongfully imprisoned, and sure, she lives with Michaela, but

Michaela…well, I've yet to decide if she can be trusted. Especially, since she'd have no problem serving my head on a silver platter to the Council of Leaders.

"What are you saying?" The question is almost too painful, too frightening to ask. Nothing can happen to Sloan. He is invincible. He has to be. But I know that no one is invincible. Not even me. Not even my mother. Not truly.

She closes her eyes as if listening. Only, I can't hear whatever she's listening for. "I need to go. The book." And just like she appeared, she's gone and I'm alone again.

I sigh, getting up from the chair and the sounds of the lapping sea come back to me. As if the sea itself had been holding its breath. What does it mean? I go back over to the book, the little flame following my movements, and rest my hand over the pages, palm flush against the rough paper.

I don't want to know. But if it can save Sloan? Bina said things were going to get difficult, but it sounds to me like things are going to get deadly. I can't bear the thought of not having Sloan by my side. The one person who's seen through all of my various layers, to the real me beneath it all. I'm not the Impossible Girl to Sloan, at least not anymore, I'm just Ka.

Before I can lose my courage, I yank out the page of the book. Bina never said that I had to read the future now. I fold it in half and then in half again so that it's small enough to fit into my palm and I close the book. Not sure what to do now, I decide to do what anyone who's done reading would do. I lift up the glass surround of the lantern and blow out the flame, engulfing myself in blackness.

My eyes fling open and at first I think I am back home, back on Xon 9 in my familiar purple bedroom. But it's only the pink light of the new dawn. I'm in the castle. My new home. Birds chirp as they awaken and an earthy aroma hits my nose. Coffee. Dad's always been an early riser. I feel the scratchiness of something in my palm and open it to see the yellowed, folded up paper resting there. I crawl to the end of the bed where a bench sits with a few t-shirts, a pair of jeans, and my messenger bag tossed rather unceremoniously. I reach into my bag and pull out a small burlap sack that Bina gave me what now seems like ages ago. Inside the sack remains only half of the original contents: a partially used pack of matches from The Old Tavern and the Sea and a small, clear crystal. The vial of acid and the speckled feather have already been used in the destruction of the Earth and Wood stones. Carefully, resisting the urge to peek at the future that awaits us in the Land of Water, I tuck the folded-up paper into the burlap sack with the matches and crystal, then toss it back into my bag before quietly padding down the steps to join my dad before everyone else wakes up.

Chapter 4

Since we arrived rather unexpectedly, none of us had any belongings. Leave it to my mother to fill everyone's closets with what seemed like an endless selection of t-shirts and jeans. But since we arrived with virtually nothing, besides the clothes on our backs and my messenger bag, that goes everywhere I do, everyone is leaving with virtually nothing too. The six of us stand beneath the pergola, a full array of exotic looking flowers are in bloom. I inhale the now familiar scents of jasmine and gardenia. They remind me of my mother and it, at least temporarily, eases my anxiety.

"Alright," my father finally says. He turns and kisses my mother's cheek and a rosy flush creeps up her neck. "I'll be back in a short while. Once, I can assure that Ahna and Li are safe and sound, I'll be back straight away."

"No heroic trips to Council Hall," my mother cautions, referring to a previous incident where we freed numerous wrongly imprisoned people kept in a secret prison.

"Wood's honor," my father replies giving her a little salute. With his tanned skin from living here, you almost wouldn't notice the brown ridges that line the side of his face. My mother—naturally— was an Earth Elemental and she used to have beautiful vines with tiny green leaves that curled up her neck and around her ear. But they're gone now that she's returned to her true form. Never able to go back. Ahna has started developing the same tiny vines, but they end just behind her ear. "Alright, kids, are we about ready then?"

"Just a minute," I say. "I want to say a proper good-bye since I don't know when…" I let my voice trail off. I don't know when—or even if—I will see my two best friends again. Sloan walks away with my parents, the tops of their heads disappearing into the garden.

The three of us stand silent. I am pretty sure that's never happened before. Best friends since we were toddlers and now so much has happened between us that it seems there is nothing left to say. Finally, Li breaks the silence.

"Well, Kata, thanks for saving my life. Again." He smirks but throws his arms around me, squeezing so hard it knocks the breath out of me and lifts my feet off the patio. This is the strongest I've seen him since the…incident, and I can't help but wonder if it has to do with his as-yet-to-be-discovered immortality. He turns us so his back is to Ahna, his tall, wide form blocking me from her line of vision. I can imagine her standing there though, with her arms crossed and eyes rolled. He scoops up my chin and looks me square in the eyes. Familiar pools of molten brown look back at me and it's been so long since I've seen that sparkle in them that my breath catches in my throat. My mother has performed a miracle. "You be safe okay? And if that slug ever hurts you, you let me deal with that."

I give him a little smile. "You and I both know Sloan would never do that."

He shrugs. "I know, but I still have to say it. Best friend and first love privilege." First love? I don't ever remember us being *that* exactly, but who knows what feelings Li's kept hidden for all these years. Just because I didn't see it the same way, doesn't make it any less valid. He leans in and kisses me on the corner of the mouth, just enough to be borderline inappropriate and make the Fire in my blood prickle to the surface. Fire and Fire is never a good combination. He pulls back and studies me carefully. I used to think the black filigree now lining his face was an imperfection—an imperfection that I had given him. But now, healthy and full of vitality again thanks to my mom, it makes him look like a warrior. "Good luck, Kata."

"Thanks," I say but the words come out bashful. Li smiles, satisfied at the effect he's had on me. Cocky as usual.

"Are you about finished, Liwald?" Ahna asks, emphasizing her twin's full name. He glowers at her and drops his arms from my waist.

I'm not sure what Ahna will do. I can feel the wedge growing between us, more so each day. Li wanders away calling out that he'll go fetch Absalom. At first I think the guard is slipping in her brown eyes, but it quickly reappears. Where Li's eyes are melted chocolate,

Ahna's are like black ice.

"Good luck," she says simply and I think that's all she's going to say, but suddenly she seems to muster up more courage. "And just because Li's obviously forgiven you, doesn't mean that I do."

I feel my heart hammering in my chest. Ahna and I never have had a fight. Ever. In almost eighteen years of friendship. Then again, maybe we are long overdue.

"It was an accident." The words sound weak as they slip from my lips. But it's still true. I carried around blame for a long time and Li was always the first to tell me it wasn't my fault. It was the fault of the Imminent Darkness. But if I wasn't around, the Imminent Darkness wouldn't be either.

"Two times, Kata. Two times you nearly killed my brother. And pretty much my only friend."

"Not your only friend." The words sting, but maybe I deserve them.

"My only friend as you run off to portals and different lands, someone is staying behind dealing with the wrath of the Imminent Darkness. The chaos and the danger that's left in its wake while you prance around retrieving magical stones. It isn't easy when you can't trust anyone. And the one person I know I can trust has almost died twice." I don't know what to say. I could say sorry, but the word seems so inadequate. Li himself even told me that I'm sorry too much and that the word serves no purpose. Words are empty. Actions show intent. She crosses her arms and regards me. I can almost feel the frigidity radiating off her. And it is so un-Ahna like.

"And don't think I don't know what your mom did."

"What?" I ask trying to play dumb. Because how could she possibly know?

"I can put two and two together. The magical elixir from the Wood stone and your mother's powers. It isn't hard to guess, especially with Li's remarkable recovery, that she's made him immortal too."

I shrug helplessly and Ahna takes it as an admission. We hear the crunch of gravel signaling the return of the others down the garden's path.

"Don't worry I won't tell him. The last thing I need is for him to try and jump off a mountain or something just to prove it. Still, it doesn't change anything." Her eyes are unsmiling but as Li emerges from the garden, with my parents and Sloan in tow, she puts on a fake smile. I feel nauseous inside and my face must show it because Sloan gives me a concerned look.

"Ready to go, Sis?"

"There's no place like home," Ahna smiles, cutting her eyes to me and giving me a final icy glare.

My father gives me a kiss on the head and then instructs Ahna and Li to link arms so that the three of them make a tiny circle. "Off we go!" he says, placing the index and middle fingers of his right hand over the watch face. In a shimmery instant they're gone as if they never were even there.

"Well, then. Let's get you two on as well," Mom says. "Time is wasting. And I may be immortal, but not everyone can afford the wait. Come inside and I'll explain to you once more how you can travel to the Land of Water and bypass the Elemental Abyss." She turns, her long dress scraping softly along the patio stones, and leads the way back into the castle.

Sloan takes my hand and from the look on his face, I can tell that he's glanced inside my head. He doesn't do it often now unless I let him, in fact he's shown me how to block it by imagining the words *NO!* in my mind's eye, but this time I don't care because I don't want to talk about it. Talking about the fact that Ahna—my truest and best friend who always believed in me—now hates my guts, would make it that much more real. And for now, I'd rather pretend it's not.

. . .

I watch my mother rather dubiously as she pulls out a large basin from a cabinet in the ginormous kitchen. Further proof that chivalry isn't dead, Sloan takes it from her hands when she struggles beneath it. She instructs him to place it on the large wooden dining table. The bowl is about as wide as a sink, but not nearly as deep. The color is a brilliant cobalt blue. It's what my mom calls stoneware, and it's also what most of our mugs, plates, and bowls back home were made of.

She comes to stand beside us holding a pitcher of water which she unceremoniously pours into the basin. The last time Sloan and I were in the Elemental Abyss one of the sea creatures in the enchanted lake warned us that it was getting dangerous, that the Imminent Darkness had been there and that not everyone could be trusted. Then, when we returned from the Land of Wood, roughly spit out the portal door, we discovered all the sea creatures that had inhabited the lake—Unbalanced Waters put their as protection by Raj and Katayun—had died. Including my friend Brooks. Everly, Brooks, almost Li. Almost Bina. Almost my mother. It's a list I'd rather didn't exist. But that seems to be getting more difficult with each journey I take.

That's why we are here now. I have my ring to return home whenever I want and it will take me to my parents, because that's what home is. Not a place, but a feeling. I look at Sloan who's peering into the basin of water, a serene expression on his face. We can have many homes.

We need to find a way to the Land of Water that bypasses the Elemental Abyss and possibly any immediate danger. Danger—as Bina so bluntly put it in my dream—is a given, but I hope that we can at least outrun it this time. There's a bundle of herbs on the table. I notice a bunch of lavender and something that has silky silver petals. I've never seen that before. My mother catches my glimpse.

"Argentum Flora Immortalis," she explains as if I have any idea what that means.

Sloan looks up from the bowl, a lock of brown hair falling across his forehead. He runs his fingers through his hair, temporarily returning it to its proper place. He looks so young in this moment. Hard to imagine the amount of responsibility that's been placed on his shoulders. And here I'm worried about me. *Even if it could save the one you love?* My heart double times at the thought of Bina's ominous words.

"Silver Flower Immortal?" he asks reaching a finger out to one of those smooth petals that seem to have a luminescence all their own.

"Very good." My mother smiles. Back home she worked in agricultural studies.

"I thought there was no such thing? Kind of like the knights of the round table and King Arthur."

"Well, obviously we know that was true. And we know that all the other myths, legends, and tales of ancient gods and goddesses were all true. So, of course, by default the Bloom of Immortality exists. And it just so happens—lucky for you two—that I grow some here in the garden."

I'm not impressed with this intellectual banter. School was never my strong suit and I'm not about to geek out over a flower, no matter how gorgeous it is. In fact, it looks as if it was picked from another planet and brought to this one. In fact, considering I haven't figured out for sure if these Lands are other planets, other dimensions, or a rift in the time space continuum, the flowers probably originated from another planet. In another galaxy. In another universe. Weirder things have happened.

"What does it do?" I ask. I like to think that I ask the important questions. You know, the obvious questions everyone else forgets about while they get all nerdy over the minute details.

My mother uses scissors to snip some lavender and I watch as the soft purple spikes drop into the pool of water. "It opens up intergalactic communications."

"What? Like some sort of telephone line for immortals?"

She smiles, her gray eyes soft, but filled with the knowledge of a hundred lifetimes. "Something like that." She finishes with the lavender, then gently stroking the Argentum Flora Immortalis, she sprinkles its petals into the bowl. The water instantly changes. Oily, metallic swirls coalesce with the lavender, pushing the earthy scent up and out so that it fills the room. I can feel the herb's effect on my anxiety almost instantaneously, which makes me wonder if the recipe—spell? concoction?—really called for it in the first place. A calmness seems to wash over me as I watch the Bloom of Immortality make its phone call.

In no time at all the water seems to slosh around inside the dish of its own accord. Like it's creating a tiny vortex in the center of the pool of water. Yet, it never rises above the rim of the bowl. Just swirls and swirls. Mother, Sloan and I peer over the bowl. Mother's expression is expectant. She's obviously done this before, but Sloan's, and I imagine my own expression, are ones of wonder. The Universe truly is bigger than I ever could have imagined. Soon the water seems to calm down, returning to stillness.

As it does, I begin to see the outline of a face. A woman with a pointy chin and angular cheekbones begins to take form in the surface of the water. She has silver eyes, like the Argentum Flora Immortalis, framed by long dark lashes. Her mouth is a puckered blue color and she has so much blonde hair that it fills the rest of the bowl where her face is not. The ends of her hair are also blue. Lining either cheek are gills similar to the ones that Sloan has on his neck. She squints as if trying to see who's on the other end of the call. Does the Universe need reception? A look of recognition crosses over her face.

"Kesara." The voice is small and light. It doesn't match the ferocity of the face that peers back at us.

"Tullia." My mother smiles. She puts an arm around me and yanks me closer to the bowl of water. "This is my daughter, Ka." I smile awkwardly and wave a hand in greeting at the face looking up at me with its unblinking silver eyes. "Ka, this is my sister, the Goddess of Water."

CHAPTER 5

"Hello, dear niece. It's a pleasure to finally meet you. Given all the trouble that your birth has caused. Quite the stir in the Universe you've made." Tullia's eyes dart to her left where Sloan stands, peering into the bowl. "Who's the handsome merman?" she asks, fluttering her long eyelashes coyly.

"The handsome merman happens to be my boyfriend," I reply slightly irritated. "And he's about a million years too young for you. Literally." I notice the pink flush that spreads over Sloan's human-skinned cheek.

"Well, I never!" scoffs Tullia.

"Ladies, please." My mother turns to me. "You'll have to excuse Tullia she's always been a bit man crazy. I think she may be part siren."

"Sirens are a myth…" Sloan begins, but my mom levels him with a look. "Oh, right. Never mind." He takes a step back from the table, so that he is standing behind my right shoulder, but if he looks over he can still see into the bowl.

My mom presses forward undeterred. "Tullia, as you know, Ka is retrieving the stones that were thrown into the Elemental Abyss. However, the Abyss seems to have been breached by the Imminent Darkness."

A shadow passes over Tullia's luminescent skin. "So I've been informed. I was saddened to hear of the loss of my brethren." I wonder if she ever truly is sad. Her face is pretty in a sort of frightening way and there's a hint of something darker behind her silvery eyes. Something I wouldn't want to be on the wrong side of, and somehow I don't think it's very difficult to get on Tullia's wrong side.

"Yes, that was a horrible loss." Mother sympathizes, then continues. "I was wondering then if you would grant Ka and Sloan passage to the Land of Water."

At this, and to my surprise, Tullia's face seems to brighten a little. "I can't help them find the stone, you know. The Impossible Girl needs to do that on her own." I hear a splash in the background and Tullia throws a glare over her shoulder. "Can't you see I have someone on the line?" she barks. She turns back around to face us. "Besides, I'd never know the first place to look."

"Thank you, Tullia. I truly appreciate it."

My aunt nods. "It's a shame we're only talking given the circumstances. It seems like forever." Her mercurial eyes get a faraway look to them then she shakes her head, blonde hair swirling around her. A lock sticks to her blue lips as she adds, "Send them on through. I'll have someone waiting." And just as easily as she appeared, Tullia's face seems to evaporate from the bowl of water.

Sloan peers over my shoulder. "It's empty."

"It is. Now that we have Tullia's blessing, we need to get you guys going on your mission. Ka, do you have your bag? Sloan?" My messenger bag goes everywhere with me. I have my map of the Elemental Abyss which I guess I no longer need, the sack from Bina, and…the page from the book in my dream. I decided to leave my copy of *The Five Elemental Goddesses,* which I'd been carrying with me, upstairs on my bed. Who knows? Maybe my mother would enjoy reading it. For old time's sake. Sloan pats the small leather satchel he has slung across his shoulders. A gift from my parents.

"All good, Mrs. Waylon."

"Wonderful. Follow me." We follow her out the front of the castle and down the stone steps toward the pink sand of the beach below. "Really, it's rather easy. Sloan, you should have little problem. With your gills, you were practically made for this. On the other hand, my dear daughter, you are going to need some extra assistance."

We reach the sandy shore. The sun is high in the sky now and the sky is a beautiful shade of turquoise. A slight breeze ruffles the hair at the back of my neck. After a little mishap involving some short circuiting, Sloan cut my hair so that it was shorter in the back with longer pieces in the front. It's finally starting to grow. The longer pieces which were once chin-length are almost to my collarbone and the back now touches the nape of my neck. Still too short for a ponytail which was my standard go to.

My mother reaches into the pocket of her long, fuchsia dress and pulls out a vial. Ever since returning home—to her true home anyways—my mother has looked more and more like a goddess. She appears in her early thirties with long, chestnut curls that cascade down her back and she's taken to wearing long skirts and dresses, something she never wore back home. Xon 9 doesn't really lend itself to frivolity. If it weren't for the depth behind her pale gray eyes, you'd never be able to tell her true age. She hands me the vial.

"Drink this." I uncork the vial and instinctively smell it. I practically choke on the sulfuric smell. "I said, *Drink this*. Not, *Smell this*."

"And for good reason too." I reply. "It smells horrible." I squeeze the tip of my nose—a trick that Li taught me—and throw back the contents of the vial like I'm doing a shot at Bernard's in the Black Bazaar. It burns all the way down hitting my stomach like I swallowed a lead brick.

My mother and Sloan watch me intently, as if they're expecting me to morph a mermaid tail right here on the beach. I am about to inform them that I feel no effects from the concoction when my stomach beings to churn. No, not churn. Bubble. I can feel the bubbles pushing up out of the contents of my stomach and up my throat, down my tongue, and then pushing against the backs of my teeth until my mouth is forced open and several bubbles escape. As they pop, they make a sound. Words. "How." "Did." "That." "Happen?" I look at my mother quizzically, a slight feeling of panic rising in my chest.

Instead of being horrified, she nods satisfied. "It's working. Just wait."

Sloan has a bemused expression on his face as he watches my transformation. I'm overcome with the feeling as though someone is stabbing me in the neck—a flashback to Li sitting behind me in Universal History poking me with his pencil—and I put my hands around my neck as if I could smother away the pain.

"Is she going to be okay?" Sloan asks, a worried edge to his voice.

"She will. Trust me. It's better than her drowning." Suddenly I feel something slimy beneath my fingers and I yank my hands away from my neck.

A small, smile creeps across Sloan's face. "You have gills."

"Gills?" I ask disbelieving. I touch my fingers to my neck and I feel the gentle movement, like the waves of the ocean.

"Now, you will be able to breathe on land or in water."

"Ka, your hands!" Sloan says and I my arms, holding my hands out in front of me, inspecting them. Thin pieces of skin have grown in between my fingers. I now have webbed-fingers. And I would assume toes too. Except I can't feel them in my boots.

"Now, it won't last forever, Ka. Once you return home it should be almost worn off. But it should last as long as you need it," my mother instructs.

"This is all fine and dandy, but what about our stuff? Sloan's new bag? Our clothes? Aren't they going to get ruined?" I ask.

My mother smiles and I can see the similarities between her and Tullia in the sharpness of her features. "I think you will find, just as in the other Lands, that some things aren't an issue. Okay, then off you go." She leans forward and kisses my cheek, then surprises me by grabbing Sloan's shoulders and kissing his cheek too. "You'll take good care of her then?"

"The best," he promises.

I shrug my shoulders and slip my new webbed hand into Sloan's. It's weird to not be able to completely intertwine my fingers with his. We begin to walk toward the sea until the cerulean water comes up and encircles our ankles.

"Oh, and one more thing!" my mother calls from behind us. We turn and she's already only a silhouette on the beach behind us. "Don't forget you are a Water Elemental, Sloan! Your body will adapt rather quickly! Oh, and watch out for the sirens! Nasty creatures!"

"That's reassuring," I mumble. I turn back around and we continue walking until my feet no longer touch the bottom. My mother told us that we were to swim out until we saw a small, bright orange buoy. That's where we are supposed to dive down and when we do we will find the portal that will take us to the Land of Water, and whoever Tullia sent to greet us.

I have to admit the webbed fingers make gliding through the water a bit easier. I've never been a good swimmer. Okay, I've never been a swimmer. Period. All I know, I've just learned in the past couple of days. I am the opposite of Sloan who swims gracefully and quickly, slicing through the water like a dancer. It's a different kind of movement than the jerky motions our bodies seem limited to when on land, like he's a bird flying, only in the water instead of the sky.

Finally, I can see something small on the horizon. "There!" I call. Sloan pauses following my extended arm and nods.

"Last one there's a stinky eel!" he sings and is off like a flash. Totally not fair and he knows it. He's just showing off. But I follow him, my heart ready to burst in my chest from swimming for such an extended period of time. He makes it seem so effortless, and even though I can see the strength and discipline that would have made him a good Metal, I can't imagine him as anything but a Water.

By the time I reach the little, orange buoy he's treading water beside it, not even out of breath. I glare at him. "Show off."

He wraps an arm around my waist. "So I want to impress my girlfriend. Is that such a crime?" He kisses me and I can taste the salt from the sea on his lips. Any irritation instantly evaporates.

"Okay, so we're here," I say still a bit dizzy from the kiss. I shake my head to try and right my brain. Sloan always seems to have that effect on me. It's strange because he used to have the opposite effect on me. As my teacher, I never understood why he seemed to watch me and pick on me, but now I understand why. For a long time, after I found out about the stones, he refused to help me and I have to admit, it was a very big source of my frustration. However, I eventually found out his Everlasting Vow couldn't interfere with my free will. When I realized he was an ally and not my enemy, it was kind of easy to see the person he was underneath it all. Our relationship feels as natural as the moon and the stars or the sea and the sand....I'll spare you the continuation of analogies, but basically I can't imagine my life without him by my side. "What now?"

He gives me a huge grin, like he's never had more fun. "We dive." And before I can lose my nerve he grabs my hand, and shoots downward into the water, pulling me along beside him. He's fast and soon the illumination of the sun is a speck in the distance behind us. I kick my legs behind me to keep up. At first I feel the pressure building up in my chest, craving air, but then I remember that I don't need it and relax into the sensation of having gills. Before us looms nothing but darkness. We continue to swim downward toward an invisible destination. Diving deeper into the murky depths of the sea.

Down.

Down.

Down.

Chapter 6

After what seems like hours, but is probably only minutes I can see a tiny white dot of light. As Sloan swims us closer it seems to grow and expand. I'm disoriented from the darkness, unable to tell what time of day it is this far from the surface. The light seems to pulsate and I realize it matches the beats of my heart. Sloan glances at me over his shoulder as if to ask, *Do you feel that?* I nod. *I do.* On my previous journeys to the other Lands the portal entrance was simply a door in the Elemental Abyss. Each door was linked to a strange, glowing sphere that seemed to search inside of you, before plucking something out of your head, and in turn opening a door. But to get home, we'd have to search for the dark, swirling mass from which we'd unceremoniously been tossed in.

Here, it feels like the opposite. We can't search for a dark swirling mass, when all around us is darkness. Instead, the light grows larger as we approach. Before our eyes, it seems to expand until it is large enough to swallow us whole. With a final glance over his shoulder, Sloan tightens his fingers—which I've noticed have now become webbed like my own—around my wrist as he picks up the pace and swims directly into the circle of white light.

The first thing I notice is that this portal contains air. I inhale and exhale deeply, savoring the sensation while I can. The next thing I notice is that I can't see. This doesn't surprise me because it was the same with the other portals. Something about traveling to the other Lands—dimensions?—whatever it is my brain can't comprehend the physics of it, robs you of your senses, but at the same time it heightens something else. For instance, since Sloan is touching me I am blasted with a barrage of thoughts and memories. I can see him watching Li warily as he says something flirtatious to me and smiles. Then it flashes to the Imminent Darkness as a wolf attacking me, using Li's life force against me. Because would I really kill my friend to save myself? And then it flashes to us swimming in the sea, me wearing nothing but a thin tank top that's pressed against my body, more revealing than I'd ever realized, as I backstroke away from Sloan, a smile on my face as I learn how to dance with the water. These images come rapid fire. I've had this experience three times: with Doran, my mom, and Sloan. I imagine it's two-way, but I am not completely sure. It feels like a gross invasion of privacy and I've never mentioned it and neither have they. These flashes seem to reveal intimate moments and even though I'm momentarily formless, I can feel the heat inside of me.

We fly through the nothingness, just blinding white light, like the blank page of a notebook. And in some ways it is, because each Land and the people—if there's people—who inhabit it are unique. It's an adventure waiting to be written. I can see a pinprick of cerulean blue growing large. Normally this would be white light because we'd be surrounded by blackness, but here it seems everything is a bit reversed. I feel Sloan's fingers tighten as he seems to brace himself. The brilliant blue light grows brighter. We hurtle toward it and I can feel myself being sucked up and in, then burped out.

And just like that I can see again. But I'm also back to relying on my new gills in order to breathe. My eyes take a minute to adjust. This is not dark and murky like the bottom of the sea in the Land of Earth. This is...different. The word magical comes to mind. Light filters in diffusing everything with a soft, glittering effervescence. There are schools of vibrantly colored fish that swim by: hot pink, tangerine, electric blue, white. Bright green grasses sway all around us.

"I thought Tullia said someone was going to greet us?" I ask. My voice comes out normal sounding enough, if not slightly more melodious.

Just then, tailing a school of fish and swimming erratically, a man approaches. He appears about Sloan's age. He has black hair that falls across his face and his eyes are lavender. His cheeks are angular and instead of in his neck, his gills are in his cheeks like Tullia's, the only difference being that where a human nose would be is just empty space. Somehow it isn't as jarring as one would think it would be. I suppose it makes sense. If you don't breathe through a nose, what's the point? The missing facial feature, doesn't make him any less handsome. His body, from the waist up is sinewy and elegant, not an inch of extraneous fat on his body. He has intricate black bands tattooed around his arms that sort of remind me of Li's facial marks. The lower half of the man's body ends in a tail that is covered in silvery green scales, similar in color to the ones that line the side of Sloan's own face.

"Sorry, I'm late!" he says as he swims up to us. His voice has the same melodious quality. I'm no science geek, but I wonder if it has to do with the surrounding water's manipulation of the sound waves. Two dolphins swim past us, close enough for me to reach out and touch, the smooth surface of their skin passing just beneath my fingertips. We may not have any of these sea creatures on Xon 9, but that doesn't mean we didn't learn about them in Earth Biology.

The merman sticks out a webbed hand. "I'm Ridge. And you must be Ka." I shake his hand with my own webbed one, and for a moment I am dizzy with a strange feeling. My heart pounds in my chest and I'm overcome with the urge to throw my arms around Ridge's neck and never let go.

Sloan bumps me out of the way and grabs Ridge's hand. "Sloan. Ka's boyfriend." And just like that the sensation is gone.

Ridge's smile doesn't budge. "Tullia's castle is this way. So if you'll just follow me." We hang back just a little behind Ridge, careful to not get whacked by his massive tail. He's a fast swimmer and I struggle to keep up, but still manage to whisper to Sloan.

"What was that?"

"Sort of an enchantment. Sirens may be able to put one over on a sailor, but mermen have their own special sort of charm. But it's through touch, not voice. As soon as I saw your pupils dilate I knew we could be in some trouble." Sloan glances at Ridge who swims effortlessly through the water. "Also, they can be quite territorial."

As much as I'm flattered that someone as hot as Ridge wants me for his own devices, I'm happy to have Sloan, especially now in a world that seems to play more by his rules than mine. We hurry to catch up with Ridge and I try to take in my surroundings. The grass has given way to stone structures interspersed with a rainbow of coral. I've never seen so many colors in one place. There are little doorways in the stone structures, the view inside blocked by curtains of dark green seaweed. I see more fish and dolphins, a giant, purple octopus swims past in the opposite direction. There are mermaids laying on top of some of the stone structures, as if they'd be sunning themselves if they were above the surface. They braid each other's hair, stopping to stare appreciatively first at Ridge as he swims past, then at Sloan. A few flutter their ridiculously long eyelashes and giggle, a sound like the tinkling of bells that choruses through the ocean. It's as if I am chopped liver. *Don't mind the human girl swimming past. Nothing to see here, folks.*

Finally, a large stone structure comes into view. It dwarfs the smaller stone structures we swam past. The castle consists of several turrets of varying heights with open windows unhindered by seaweed curtains. Stone archways and columns complete the effect. At the top, a purple flag with a white wave cresting over, flaps in the current. There are stone steps and tall, tubular magenta grass that seem to encircle the castle like a natural fence. Ridge pauses and turns to us.

"Welcome to the home of Tullia, Queen of the Land of Water," he says gesturing proudly as if the castle is his personally. His lavender eyes sparkle with what I can only interpret as loyalty and love for her majesty.

Sloan and I exchange a look. *Queen?* Apparently, goddess isn't enough, so she has also deemed herself a Royal Highness. I wonder what Raj and Katayun think about that. Still, I suppose queen of the entire Universe trumps queen of only a single element. I swallow the nervous feeling that has begun to rise in my stomach. Somehow, I feel ill-equipped to deal with my aunt. And her ego.

Before we can say anything in reply, Ridge turns again and swims head first disappearing through the pink seagrass. Without much choice, we follow him.

. . .

Truth be told the pink sea grass isn't as much a fence as a decoration. It almost tickles as we swim through it. Rainbow-colored flowers wave in greeting, rocking back and forth along with the current. We come to a stop at a door. Unlike the stone homes with seaweed doorways that we swam past, Tullia's castle door is made entirely of a shiny, opalescent material.

Ridge looks at us proudly. "The Queen's door is made out of the interior of conch shells, painstakingly created by one of our master craftsmen."

I look at Sloan as if to say, *Of course it is.* But instead of a companionable eye roll, there's a dark tint to Sloan's eyes and his brow is furrowed. I've known him long enough to know that this means he feels something is wrong or off. I put a webbed hand on his forearm. This is my aunt we're talking about, and as aloof as she seemed upon first meeting, she's still family. He looks at me and nods, but I can see that his eyes are still concerned.

The door is guarded by another merman. Although, he's not as pleasant looking as Ridge. Sure, he has muscles on his muscles, but his face is stony and he holds a trident. He also has tattoos that wind all over his body, letters and symbols twisting every which way, none of which makes any sense to me. And I wonder for the first time, if perhaps English isn't the only language in this Land. I remember in Human Evolution taught by Teacher 36, that we started out as tiny microbes in the sea. If that were true, then it's possible that these sea people—sea worlds—have been here for a long time. As long as the Universe, I would guess. Ancient people. Ancient languages. No wonder it's all gone to Tullia's head.

The guard glowers at us. His grip tightens on his trident. Ridge scowls at him. "Relax, Nightfall. This is the Queen's niece and her companion." This does little to reassure Nightfall that we aren't a threat. Ridge lowers his voice even though Nightfall could still easily hear him. "He takes his job very seriously."

Nightfall ignores us while Ridge waits patiently as the shell door lowers, like a drawbridge. Even though there's no moat. Or is it all moat? It's hard to tell.

"Is his name really Nightfall?" I ask.

"No, it's George." Ridge smirks. I glance at Nightfall and his right eye seems to twitch. I do believe he wants to punch Ridge in his pretty, little face.

"I see why he went with Nightfall then," I say. We swim into the entryway of the castle and as much as I thought no one could top my mom's castle, Tullia has come close. The ceilings are high and there's a grand staircase with orange, pink, green, and purple fish swimming about as if they're on some very important task. And for all I know, maybe they are. The stairs wrap around from either side of the entryway, meeting in the middle where above hangs an elaborate chandelier made out of thin pieces of shell with tiny twinkling lights.

"The lights are little sea worms that glow," Ridge informs us. With how much excitement he has for this place, you'd think that he'd built it from the ground up himself.

There are white statues along the walls, maybe twelve in total. I peer closely as we pass and notice each one appears to be a male. A human male. They all look young, and handsome. For a statue. In the center of the staircase where it curves to meet, and beneath the chandelier, is a fountain. The irony is not lost on me that there is a fountain underwater. Nevertheless, it is circular and in the center is a curvaceous woman. She has a mermaid tail and is naked from the waist up. The sculptor was quite generous in the female anatomy department it would seem. Long hair curls over and around the statue's breasts, and the pixie like jawline is thrust upward toward the ceiling. Long, lithe arms are above her head as if she's dancing. Water shoots out of her mouth and up into the air.

We float up the staircase and from above I can see that the mermaid in the fountain is—who else?—Tullia. Guess modesty is not something she shares in common with my mother. Sloan's eyes look as if they are going to bug out of his head, but Ridge swims on as if this isn't the weirdest place ever. It's like a tribute to Tullia.

"Who are the guys?" I ask gesturing behind me to the statues.

Ridge shrugs as if it doesn't really matter who they are. "Suitors of Tullia. She's had many."

"There were only twelve statues," Sloan says.

"Yes, in *this* room." Ridge laughs as if the joke's somehow on us. "You'll find that the statues line all of the castle hallways as well. Men find Tullia…irresistible." He puts a strange emphasis on the word irresistible and, given what little I know of Tullia, I can't help but wonder how many of those found her irresistible of their own accord. Obviously, Ridge finds her so. Then again I have a hunch that Ridge would find anything with breasts irresistible.

At the top of the staircase there's an entrance and we follow a short hallway—lined with portraits in golden frames of Tullia no less—that spills open onto a large room. From the ceiling hang several purple banners. The center one has the same cresting wave as the flag outside. This banner is by far the largest of the five. On both sides of the large banner are two shorter banners, and I recognize the symbolism almost immediately. There's a white flame, a tree, a round globe, and a lightning bolt. The drawings may be primitive, but I recognize them as the Elements. *See?* I mouth to Sloan. At least she's honoring her sisters. But he still looks unsure.

On the floor is a long, golden-colored rug. On closer inspection, I realize it isn't golden-colored, it is actual gold. In the form of coins and they are somehow sewn together to form a runner. How did she get these gold coins? Is it the Land's own currency? They almost remind me of a pirate's treasure chest. We read *Treasure Island* and *Peter Pan* in school, so I feel I am well-versed enough in the Old Earth lore to suspect the possibility. But how did it get here?

The room seems to go on forever until we reach the end, where stand two more merman, both with the same strange tattoos as the guard outside. I wonder about the meaning of the tattoos. These merman are also holding tridents and they don't make eye contact with any of us as we pass. Suddenly, I realize that Ridge is Tullia's servant...or henchman. The way the guards ignore him, not even sparing him a glance. And also Nightfall's irritation with him. Not to mention, Ridge's seeming infatuation with his queen.

Just past the guards is a huge throne made of—what else?— seashells. Although this time the shells are of varying shapes and sizes somehow stuck together to form a ridiculously large and elaborate chair. On either side of the throne is a colorful, clay vase full of glowing flowers, but as we get closer I realize that they're moving. And blinking. Perhaps more of the sea worms. For once, I wonder why Ridge isn't offering us a full-on history of the plants— animals?—in the vases. But then I realize it's because Tullia is perched upon the throne, looking tiny and delicate in its largeness.

Like her sculpture doppelganger, she has a long, scaled tail that's an opalescent purple color. Unlike her sculpture doppelganger, she's covered up more or less because her scales don't stop at her bellybutton, but run all the way up and over her chest before dispersing along her neck and shoulders. Her long blonde hair floats around her head like its own crown, blue tips forming a wild halo. Her blue lips are small and puckered and even from several feet away her silver eyes are piercing. She's terrifyingly beautiful. Emphasis on the terrifying.

"Niece," she says by way of greeting. Her voice has the same sing-song quality, but it sounds more baritone than soprano, not matching the petite sea creature that lounges across the throne. The body language says *don't care*, but the glint in her eyes and the slight curl to her upper lip convey something else.

I know she is expecting me to say, *Majesty*. Or *Your Royal Highness*. Which my friends joked about when they found out I was half-immortal and a grand-daughter to Raj and Katayun, the true King and Queen of the Universe. But there's only room for one, I think. So as a compromise, I do an awkward curtesy of sorts and bow my head, biting my lip as I reply.

"Hello, Aunt."

I hear Ridge's sharp intake of breath beside me. At that moment, I can almost feel Sloan inside my head, instead of reading my thoughts, inserting his own. *This isn't going to go well.*

CHAPTER 7

Tullia's smile tightens, blue lips framing sharp, pointed teeth. I blink and they're gone, replaced with perfect, pearly whites. But her eyes betray the smile and I realize I may not have imagined the snarl after all. Stranger things have happened.

Ignoring my greeting, she gestures at the room. "So what do you think of my castle?"

I hesitate. I want to say, "You mean *An Ode to a Narcissist?*" Instead I say, "It's beautiful. I love the banners. It's a nice touch." Which makes me feel good because it isn't even a half-truth, it's the honest truth. The castle is like nothing I've ever seen before. And if it didn't have all the pictures and statues of Tullia on every wall and in every corner, it would be quite lovely.

"I'm glad you like it. How about you, Handsome?" She turns her mercurial eyes on Sloan, her pupils narrow pinpricks.

"It's wonderful, Your Majesty. A true reflection of your own beauty." He bows to her slightly and I kind of want to vomit on the superfluous gold-coin rug. But I don't want to ruin my boots. *Suck up*, I think.

Tullia smiles wide, a dimple popping out in her left cheek. "You have impeccable taste." She glances at me and I look over at Ridge, who is studying the animal-plant beside the throne intensely. "Or so it would seem." *Was that a dig?* I feel like maybe I should be insulted.

"Indeed. I'm a lucky girl," I say through clenched teeth, and I see the twitch of a smile at Sloan's lips as he rises from his bow.

Deciding she's had enough for now, Tullia waves a hand at Ridge, drawing back his attention. He looks at her eagerly, as if there is nothing that would please him more than to serve his queen. "Take my niece and her companion to the guest chambers. I think I'm in a need of a nap before dinner." She lets out an exaggerated yawn, raising her arms above her head, her blonde hair moving slightly and, despite the scales, I can't help feeling like maybe she should put on a blouse. Or better yet a turtleneck.

Ridge nods his head. "Yes, my Queen."

We follow him back the way we came, and if I weren't so paranoid I could swear Tullia is behind me throwing daggers at my back with her eyes. At least they aren't real ones. Yet.

. . .

The guest chambers are practically a whole other castle. They're on the floor above the throne room, we had to take a crystalline elevator just to get here. The rooms are probably quadruple the size of my bedroom back on Xon 9, complete with their own bathrooms Do mermen and mermaids use toilets, or are they strictly for human visitors? And if so, exactly how many human visitors is Tullia entertaining? My mind drifts to the male statues downstairs. All human. The skin on the back of my neck prickles.

"Alright then, my Lovely—" Ridge begins after we drop Sloan off at his room.

"Ka's fine." I interrupt. I can't go around having someone call me Lovely. It's just wrong on so many levels.

"Okay, then *Ka*, this is your chamber. You may rest up—and clean up—before dinner which is promptly served at seven. There's a clock on the mantle." He lowers his voice as if sharing a secret. "And Tullia *hates* to be kept waiting for dinner."

"Got it. Punctuality."

"Great. Let me know if you need anything. Just use the seahorse." With that he smiles and swims away.

Just use the seahorse? Wait. Was he implying that I am not clean? We are in water for heaven's sake! How could I not be clean? Ridge has shut the door on his way out and my eyes scan the room. There's a large bed with a pale, yellow canopy. The wood is dark and the design ornate, almost as though it's carved to look like waves. Across from the bed is a fireplace and I see the clock carved out of a white seashell. According to the clock, and this Land, it is five o'clock. I have two hours. And apparently, her Royal Highness cannot be kept waiting if she's hungry. I wonder what merpeople eat? Fish? Seems like a conflict of interest.

My eyes take in the large tapestry on the far wall, tucked between two round windows that look out into the sea. Naturally, the tapestry is a woven artwork of none other than Tullia. Here, she's depicted as human complete with legs…and everything else. Because of course she wouldn't be wearing clothes as a human either. A narcissist and a nudist. She has a whimsical expression on her face, as if she's pining away for something that's not included in the portrait. Her body is smooth and slender, all curves with no angles. Instead of a puckered blue mouth, she has plump, cherry lips, but the silver eyes remain the same.

"The artist was a bit generous, don't you think?" A voice startles me, but when I whirl around it's only Sloan.

I turn into him, as he wraps his arms around my waist. I like the sound of his voice with the melodious quality to it. It carries through the water like a little musical gift, soft and soothing.

"You could say that," I say.

"I think your aunt has some issues." He nuzzles my neck.

"Nobody's perfect," I reply. He lowers his mouth to mine and immediately my Fire lights deep in the pit of my stomach, the warmth spreading rapidly to every part of my body as if it wants to burn me up from the inside out. Lately, Sloan has seemed to have this affect me. It would appear the deeper our connection grows, the more pronounced my physiological reaction. Fire and Water. He bites my bottom lip and I let out a happy moan as he pulls me onto the oversized bed. I smile and pull away slightly, trying to regain some composure. "How'd you get in here anyways?"

He nods behind him and I see an open door. "The rooms are connected."

"How convenient."

"Very." He runs his lips over my neck and my fingers curl into his hair. Something feels different. In a good way. But not the usual. I push Sloan away gently and he lifts his head, brown hair falling into his green eyes, well, what I can see of his green eyes, because his pupils are so huge they seem to all but take up his irises.

"Are you okay?" I ask.

He grins dreamily. "I think so. Why?"

"Your eyes...seem different. That's all."

He rolls me over so that I'm lying on my back beside him. Resigned to me putting the brakes on wherever we were headed. "I guess I feel a bit different here. It's..." He shakes his head. "It's nothing."

But it is something and I could feel it. The primal urge of his desire. His face looks so serious now, pupils shrinking slightly. *Don't forget you're a Water Elemental, Sloan. Your body will adapt rather quickly!* My mother's words pop into my head. I assumed she meant adapt physically, but maybe there's more to being a merman than that. I think of the way Ridge regards Tullia, all puppy dog eyes shooting hearts and rainbows. But the way Sloan was looking at me...was different than that. Trying to lighten the mood that I more or less just ruined, I say half-jokingly, "Maybe it's all the naked pictures of my aunt."

Sloan's eyes darken again, but just as quickly lighten back up.

"I'm pretty sure it's not those. I like my women human." He glances up at the tapestry. "All of the time." He kisses my cheek and places an arm beneath my head. "Your aunt sure isn't anything like your mother."

"I suppose that's to be expected. I mean look at Li and Ahna. They're as different as night and day."

I feel Sloan's head nod, moving softly against my arm. The closeness between us sends little currents of electricity through me. Things feel strange here, and I've yet to decide if they are good strange or bad strange. There's a muffled noise and Sloan sits up looking at me quizzically. I shrug. We listen, but hear nothing. Then just as Sloan rests his head back against my arm, curling into me, we hear it again. This time there's no denying it. A soft neighing sound. Back home we don't have animals just to have animals. They're used as a food source and kept in controlled conditions. Before traveling to the Lands of Earth and Wood, I'd never interacted with wild animals: rabbits, squirrels, birds, fish, butterflies…The sound reminds me of something, but I can't think of what.

Sloan scoots off the bed and follows the sound to the corner of the room, near the ridiculously large bathroom complete with fancy, gold-footed tub and mirrored wall. "I think I found the source of the noise." He turns back toward me and in his cupped hands he is holding a tiny little creature that has the head of a horse, with a long flowing mane, but a scaled body with a curlicue of a tale. It whinnies just like a horse would. It's the sea horse, Ridge had mentioned.

I reach out a tentative finger and he nuzzles his nose against it.

"Ridge said if I needed him to just use the sea horse."

"They must be like little messengers. From what I recall from University, sea horses are quite fast."

"And adorable." Suddenly, I feel a sharp pinch and a droplet of blood floats up in the water between Sloan and me. My blood. "It bit me!" I stick my finger in my mouth. The seahorse gives me an abashed expression before floating back to its corner. I inspect my finger. Almost as soon as it had started, the bleeding has stopped.

"Well, they are wild creatures, I guess," Sloan says, double-checking the microscopic bite mark. He glances at the seashell clock behind me. "Almost six o'clock. Guess we should get ready for dinner. Ridge told me Tullia hates to be kept waiting."

"What doesn't Tullia hate?" I ask.

"You mean besides herself?" Sloan laughs as he disappears into the open door that connects our two rooms. I take a deep breath, trying to steel myself for a dinner in the same room as Tullia. We won't be staying here long. Tomorrow morning we'll be leaving because we have a stone to find. But we may as well enjoy the lavish surroundings while we have them because who knows what will be waiting for us out there, in a Land where things appear to be both mesmerizing and dangerous.

CHAPTER 8

The dining hall is a long, narrow room with an equally long, and narrow table running down the center. Above the table are three seashell and glow worm chandeliers, casting the room in rainbows of color because, of course, the room is made out of opalescent seashells. The effect is stunning, if not for the queen that sits perched at the head of the table. Sloan guides me by the elbow, placing me in a seat to Tullia's left. He takes the seat across from me. The place settings are all gold—silken golden placemats and gold dinnerware. A gold goblet filled with a ruby red liquid sits to my right. I feel my stomach clench.

Tullia picks up her own goblet, waving it around precariously. "So, what do you think?" I could play the game, filling Tullia's head with nonsense. It seems that's what everyone else does, most likely out of fear—or strange adoration. But that's not me. I don't play the game. I didn't play it with the Fairy King and I didn't play it with the Imminent Darkness, and I sure as hell am not going to play it with the Water Queen.

I am just about to comment how it's the only room without a sculpture, painting, or tapestry dedicated to Tullia's incomparable beauty, when I notice in the center of the table, down from my left is a huge sculpture. I don't know how I missed it when we walked in. I guess overtaken by the rainbow effect. The sculpture is of Tullia—naturally—and the far end is her mermaid tale curved up and apparently turned into a vase that overspills with coral and colorful flowers. She's laying on her side, her hand propping up her head, hair sculpted into a wavy crown around her head. The statue's breasts appear hollowed out and more colorful flowers spill over their rims. The ridiculousness of it all almost renders me speechless. Almost.

"A little lavish don't you think?" I say a little more snarkily than I intended.

I hear the sharp intake of breath again. And notice Ridge standing in between Sloan and Tullia at the corner of the table. When did he get here? Or was he always standing there and I just didn't notice? His lavender eyes are wide. But Tullia only laughs and I see Ridge's muscular shoulders relax.

"Is there any other way?" She titters as several mermaids, all with long brown hair tied up in braids and ribbons enter into the room carrying gold platters. The mermaids have dark blue-green scales that run from the tip of their tails all the way to the top of their heads. Silvery eyes look vacant as they stand off to the side and wait for

Tullia to command them. Tullia gestures for the mermaid-servants to bring the platters which are covered with green seaweed looking plants and fish of varying sizes. All of the fish still have their eyeballs. I feel my stomach lurch. I avert my eyes to the mermaids who, like Tullia, are pretty in a terrifying sort of way. They remind me of my friend Brooks, who lived in the enchanted lake. And who is now dead. It reminds me of the true reason I am here.

"So, what about this stone? I know you said you can't help me find it, but surely you could send us in the right direction?" I stare at the plate in front of me, a silvery fish with a rainbow belly stares blankly back at me. The bile in my stomach rises and I glance at the goblet of red liquid, but it reminds me too much of blood. I glance up at Sloan who actually looks a little green along the gills.

Tullia cuts a chunk of fish, its insides pink and meaty and shoves the forkful into her mouth. "It's around somewhere."

I nod slowly, as if I'm dealing with a small child, and I suppose in some ways that I am. "That's a start. How about what's it look like?"

Ridge continues to stand at Tullia's elbow, making sure her goblet is full and that her plate is never empty. She's already finished off an entire fish and is on her second. I wonder where she puts it all. Not like she can hide in an over-sized hoodie on a fat day. She spears a piece of slimy, fern-colored seaweed and then proceeds to twirl it around her fork like its spaghetti.

"I think it was opal." My mind flashes back to the memory of Bina giving the stones to my mother. The stones were gifts—I never knew exactly how they ended up in Bina's safekeeping, but the

Universe works in mysterious ways. It strikes me that almost everything we've seen since we've arrived has been opal.

"That's…helpful," Sloan says, using his fork to push the fish around on his plate. An eyeball bugs out and I see Sloan purse his lips tight. If worse came to worse he could always throw up in the goblet.

"I don't really remember. Blah, blah. Anuja. Blah,blah. New baby. Gift. Yadda, yadda, yadda."

Tullia's taken up the goblet again and is waving it around her head. Some of the liquid sloshes out and slowly slides down her shoulder. Then, as if it is as normal as anything, a long, black forked-tongue flickers out from between her perfect, blue lips and laps up the offending red drops, before quickly recoiling. My heart pounds in my chest. Sloan looks like he's about to be sick. Ridge looks like he's fallen in love. Tullia continues, as if the weirdest thing in the world didn't just happen.

"I know you're important and all, Ka, but my life just doesn't revolve around a baby, let alone a half-human one. Sorry, I can't be of more help."

Back home, that bully I mentioned earlier, Diadona, was always giving me backhanded compliments. Her hair was perfect and blonde, never a stray hair out of place. She would bat her eyes at Sloan—back then I only knew him as Teacher 4—and then just as sweetly as she'd answer a question in class, she'd turn to me with the same sugary smile and proceed to spit venom. Tullia reminds me of Diadona.

I'm a bit unnerved by the tongue episode, so I nod. "Yeah. No. I mean, I understand. So far you've been really helpful," I lie pulling out each word as if it pains me to say it. I glance at Sloan. "Well, dinner has been amazing, Aunt Tullia, but Sloan and I are beat and we have a big day tomorrow…going to find a seashell looking stone in an entire world full of seashells."

Sloan nods enthusiastically. "Yep, that's right. I am beat!" He leaps to his feet nearly clattering his golden dishes to the floor.

Tullia looks saddened for a moment, her blue lips forming a pout. "But you haven't even had dessert, yet!"

I grimace. "Maybe next time."

. . .

I'm curled up in Sloan's bed with his chest pressed against my back. His forehead rests against the back of my neck. Lucky for him, his room only has an oil painting of Tullia, above the fireplace. And also lucky, she's fully clothed in the painting. In fact, she's wearing an absurd hot pink ball gown, like some sort of princess. Which I guess, technically, is what she is. Even though she doesn't look old now, in the portrait she looks to be a young girl.

"This place is so strange," I whisper. We're alone as far as I can tell. No seahorses hiding in the corners. I made Sloan check. There are no lights—or creatures—turned on, but there's still a soft glow that drifts in from the windows. And I wonder if we were to float to the top of the sea, would we break the surface and find the sun and sky? It's hard to say in these types of places that seem to have their own rules. Not all of them logical. Or based in reality. My stomach growls despite the nutrient pills that we swallowed when we returned from dinner. We eat regular food on Xon 9, but sometimes you just can't be bothered to prepare a meal and the pills deliver nutrients much more efficiently.

"I kind of like it," Sloan says into the back of my neck. I turn over so that I'm facing him. His eyes are calm and his pupils have returned to normal size. I'm not sure what I saw earlier, but part of me knows it wasn't normal. Maybe not even possible. It wasn't just the physical wanting. It felt different. It was hungry. I push the thought aside. Maybe it's just this place, and I'm caught up in the weirdness of Tullia and the castle.

"You like Tullia?" I ask.

"No. You said this place. Not this person. I kind of like this place. Not the castle, of course. That's just down right ludicrous. But the Land of Water. I'd like to see more." He closes his eyes and gives me a small kiss in between each sentence.

"Well, we'll definitely see more. Tullia was about as helpful as a fish on land."

"I resemble that remark."

I giggle. And tuck my head beneath his chin. "You know what I mean." I can feel my eyes growing heavy with fatigue. This place may be strange, but at least in this moment, cocooned in Sloan's arms I feel safe. Nothing dangerous can happen with Sloan protecting me. My eyes slide closed.

"Don't worry, Kata," Sloan whispers sleepily. "We'll find it."

. . .

I'm back home. The twin moons are high in the sky and the never-setting sun casts a warm, pink glow. The temperature on Xon 9 is always a pleasant 67 degrees with a warm breeze. I'm standing outside the house I grew up in. The concrete the same terracotta red as the surrounding landscape. The house is dark, as it should be. Because no one is home. And most likely, no one will ever be home again.

There's no one around and then I remember Ahna mentioning something about a curfew. There was a curfew before, for underagers. But this curfew was different. It was for everyone. If that wouldn't make the colonists grow suspicious of the Council Leaders I'm not sure what would. I turn to the left where only a few dozen steps away is the Solloman household. On the outside it looks identical to my own. No lights are on. Except.

I notice a soft glowing light coming from deep within the belly of the house. My memory takes me back to the little tower fortress on the beach in my other dream. I know this too is a dream, but with me a dream is never only a dream. It's a message. Or a warning.

I head toward the house, my boots crunching over the dirt and silvery grass of the small front lawn. In the stillness around me, the sound is like glass shattering. I hurry as quickly as I can, slipping in between our two houses and heading toward the narrow back yard.

So many afternoons were spent playing here. Playing make believe. Good guys versus bad guys. Except now the game is reality and not make believe. Behind the house is a turned over, wooden crate. I pick it up, scanning the back of the house. Behind me are some trees, gnarled branches and chlorophyll-less leaves. The light is coming from a window just above my head. Li's bedroom. Ahna's bedroom was in the front of the house like mine. The houses are two stories and even if I stand on the crate, I won't be tall enough to look in the window. I turn back and look at the tree line, then make a slow semi-circle so that I'm facing my house. And the tree that separates my family's property from the Solloman property. That's when I get the dumbest idea ever.

I decide to climb the tree. I toss the crate back into the grass and hoist myself up using the lower branches of the tree. I wrap an arm around the trunk and stand on tiptoe reaching for the next branches. These are the branches that end near the window. The foliage above me provides cover as I inch my way along a branch, arms wrapped around as if hanging on for dear life. I've wondered before if you can die in a dream, so far my answer is no, but I'm not totally willing to try it out a second time.

Finally, I'm close enough that I can see into the window, which is easy, because Li being Li has the curtains open. He's standing shirtless and in boxer shorts staring at himself in a mirror above his dresser. The bed is unmade and there are books scattered everywhere, some open, some closed, which in itself is weird because Li is not the bookish one, in case you haven't figured that out yet. My heart leaps a little at the sight of him, my pulse quickening as the familiar, warm fire tickles the pit of my stomach. I wrap my arms tighter around the tree branch, the bark pushing sharply into my skin.

He appears to be talking to himself. The side of his face where the filigree of Fire should be is turned toward me, the black, tribal-like design clawing at his cheek. Usually, I feel sick with guilt at the sight of it, but this time I don't. Curled around the tree watching him, his shoulders thrown back, the jauntiness of his jaw, and his sinewy muscles, he looks like a warrior. My memory flashes to holding his hand as I thought he was dying, the vision of him with a bow and arrow, a red-haired girl beside him. The stones aren't the only gifts. Each stone returns some sort of special power to me. My Wood gift was a sort of time lapse, like a tree that grows from a sapling to old age, I could touch someone and see a flash of their life. Over in seconds. The other person none the wiser. I don't really like it as it seems like a gross invasion of privacy. I don't know who the red-haired girl in my vision is and it doesn't seem important now, so I push the thought aside.

Suddenly, Li's shoulders soften. He runs a hand through his black hair and begins to inspect himself in the mirror, flexing and unflexing his biceps, hardening his muscles to make his six-pack more prominent. I roll my eyes and practically fall out of the tree. That is just so typical. I steady myself with a slow breath. Li pauses and glances toward the window. I feel frozen. What if he sees me? Wait, what does it matter if this is a dream? Unless this isn't a dream. That's not confusing or anything. But maybe I'm the one dream walking for once. He shrugs and throws himself onto the unmade bed.

I wish I could see what the books are about, but I'm too far away. However, as if in answer to my wishing, Li picks up one of the books. I catch a glimpse of the title. *The Immortals*. My eyes widen and for the second time I almost fall out of the tree, but just as I begin to tumble my instincts kick in and the vines that run along my veins shoot out of the slits in my wrist and wrap around the tree, allowing me to pull myself back up. I sit up, allowing the vines to snap off, dissolving into nothing before they hit the ground. Another gift, but this one from Earth. Thanks, Mom. But that book. Does that mean that Ahna told Li what happened?

I remember her scrounged up face, her cheeks flushed with anger. Her eyes were shooting me with daggers of hatred. How is it someone I'd loved for so long could now seem to hate me so much? My stomach clenches at the thought. No, even if she hated me Ahna wouldn't tell Li. Telling Li he's immortal would be like…like telling Tullia all her sculptures and paintings are hideous. The result would most likely be catastrophic. I watch as Li turns the book so that I can no longer see its cover. The back is just plain, black leather. I sigh. This dream hasn't been very helpful. As nice as it is to see Li half-naked and making faces at himself in the mirror.

Just then Ahna appears in the open doorway. She's no longer wearing a scowl. Instead, she is wearing pink, floral pajamas. In fact she looks happy and I feel a pang of sadness. I'm the one who caused that scowl. I used to be her trusted friend and confidante, but that bond has been broken. Now, she thinks Li is all that she has left. I watch as she hands him a glass of something, then sits on the edge of the bed. She glances at some of the books and her brow furrows. No, Ahna is not the one who told Li. As quickly as the worried look appears it's gone, replaced with something else. I can't hear what they're saying, but Ahna smiles and gets up to leave. It looks like she's saying good-night. Li waves her off, engrossed with his book. So very un-Li like.

As Ahna leaves, she pauses and glances over her shoulder and through the small window. She looks right at me, eyes narrowed. I go completely still. She sees me. I can feel it in every inch of my body as every single hair follicle stands on end. Even from here I can see her brown eyes staring right through me and just before she turns around I see a flash of yellow. And that's when I really do fall out of the tree.

Chapter 9

When I roll off the bed, bracing myself for the impact of hitting the ground, I remember that I'm in a land made of water. I dolphin roll so that I'm facing back up. My acrobatics have woken up Sloan who looks at me with one eye, a green-scaled arm flung across his forehead.

Wait.

I move closer kneeling on the bed, pulling his arm and holding it out to inspect it. "When did you get more scales?" I ask trying to remain calm.

He pushes himself up to a seated position and turns his arm left then right, examining it carefully. "I didn't."

I laugh uneasily. "Well, obviously you did." I run my finger down the right side of his face and along the side of his neck. Instinctively, he closes his eyes, leaning into my touch. I continue to trace over his collarbone and then down his shoulder, along his bicep, over his forearm, and down to his webbed fingers.

"Kata." It's a warning more than anything. But I'm not trying to be sensual here. I'm trying to figure out what the heck is going on. *Don't forget you are a Water Elemental, Sloan! Your body will adapt rather quickly!*

"You're adapting."

He opens a green eye to regard me. "What?"

"You're a Water Elemental. You're body's adapting to being in its element. Literally."

He inspects his arm again. Flexing and unflexing it, like Li in my dream. Then he puts both arms out in front of him as if comparing them. One is silvery-green scaled, fading away where his shoulder joins his chest. The other is smooth and fair-colored with fine brown hairs along the forearm.

"I guess I am."

"I guess you are." I echo. I don't voice the concern that's hanging like a curtain in between us, my knee pressed into his hipbone, heart silently pounding in my chest. I try to block my thoughts, but am not sure that I'm successful when I think, *But what if you don't change back? There's no surface water on Xon 9. What if you can't come home? What will happen then?*

. . .

Somehow we are fortunate enough to not be graced with Tullia's presence this morning. Apparently, she's a late riser. Can't say that I'm surprised. Ridge is waiting outside with Nightfall. I give him a big smile.

"Good morning, George!" He glances at me and, even though he doesn't smile, there's the slightest hint of a sparkle in his eye. If I didn't know any better, I'd think he likes me. Well, maybe not like. Maybe tolerate. At least more than he tolerates Ridge.

Ridge puts an arm on my shoulder. "Before you go, the queen wanted to give you one of her water dragons."

"Wait. What?"

"A water dragon." He looks at me like I'm a simpleton. "You mean you've never heard of one before?"

Sloan explains, "It's like a horse. But not. Water dragon is a bit of a misnomer, but sea horse was already taken."

"Don't remind me," I say eyeing the scar that's formed on my index finger from that little bugger.

"I'll go fetch him. Just wait here." Ridge glances at Nightfall. "And stay out of trouble for just five minutes." He swims away disappearing around the castle.

I suppose Nightfall got his name because his hair is long and jet black, falling to his shoulders. His tattoos of curious letters and symbols seems to glow and dance around on his skin. I hadn't noticed that before.

"What's with the tats?" I ask him.

He looks at me, eyes narrowed. Clearly evaluating whether or not I can be trusted. His eyes dart to Sloan, who is obviously some sort of merman hybrid at this point, and he nods as if deciding I can be trusted.

"It's an enchantment."

"Who put it there?"

"Tullia."

"Why?"

"Is this twenty questions?"

"Why?" I press, more insistent.

Night fall sighs. "It's her way of, how should I put it? Showing what's hers?" I watch as a glowing eye and a cross with a loop move around what looks like a letter L.

"You're a slave, then?" I ask, my voice barely a whisper. I thought Tullia was terrifying, mostly because she is so full of herself, but this sheds an entirely different light on things.

"More like a conquest." I tilt my head to the side, and it takes me a moment to realize what he's implying. My memory flashes to the entryway full of human-male statues. Was Nightfall once human? His name is George. I shiver involuntarily. Nightfall lowers his voice. "You seek the Water stone, yes?"

I nod, unable to find words because what do you say to someone who was once human and now is not? It changes the way you look at someone when you realize their past was maybe not so different from your own. "Yes."

"There's a graveyard not far from here. Just past the edge of the reef. That would be the place to check."

At this point Sloan, who has been listening, joins the conversation. "A graveyard?"

"A ship graveyard." I almost can't handle this. My mother said sirens were nasty creatures. And Tullia is obviously a siren. She said she only thought Tullia was part siren. But the evidence proves otherwise. My mother also failed to mention that sirens were dangerous.

Nightfall notices the wave of understanding that passes over my face. "Yes."

"For how long?"

"Centuries." I reach out a hand and place it on his forearm, which is so muscular, my webbed fingers don't even wrap around. Sometimes the words left unspoken can have the most impact.

Ridge comes back around the corner just as I pull my hand away. He looks like a little boy sitting atop a large creature that looks to be part horse and part eel. The head is angular with long tendrils near its mouth a wide ridged-crown that acts like a mane. The body is all eel with some ridged fins on either side. The beast's color is a mixture of reds and blues, coalescing to various shades of purple in some spots. He's beautiful.

Ridge slides down from his perch behind the creature's neck. "This is Altair." At the mention of his name, the sea dragon lowers his head as if bowing in greeting.

"This is what Tullia considers a gift?"

"She is a generous queen," Ridge replies automatically. I can see Nightfall stifle a snort. Ridge has tattoos too and I notice that his do not move. There's no arranging and rearranging like the ones that adorn Nightfall's body. Maybe that's not the only difference between the two. Maybe it means that Ridge was never human. Ignoring

Nightfall's near snort, which apparently Ridge has grown accustomed to, he continues. "Altair is our finest and strongest sea dragon. You should fare well in his care."

Altair pulls himself up to his full height, black eyes gleaming proudly. I think this animal may have more brain cells than Ridge. And that's a good sign. Sloan is already scrambling up to Altair's neck and he reaches a hand down to help me up. I left my boots behind. They were heavy and burdensome, and now my toes match my fingers as I suspected. Webbed. Sloan wraps his arm around mine, grabbing at the forearm and pulls me up easily. I scooch in behind him, wrapping my arms around his waist but not before first giving Altair a gentle pat on the neck to say hello.

"Well, I hate long good-byes," Ridge says. "So, off you go." He pulls a hanky out of…I'm not sure where and begins to dab at his lavender eyes.

I roll my eyes and catch Nightfall rolling his at the same time. Poor guy isn't only stuck as a merman trapped here by Tullia, but he also has to put up with Ridge. Every. Single. Day. That in itself seems torturous. And I've only been here a day.

Sloan whispers something and Altair rears up a little, then surges forward and I feel myself thrown backwards a little, holding onto Sloan's waist so that I don't slide off. My messenger bag is secure behind me. And we're flying. This isn't the first time I've flown though. My Aunt Constancia took bird form and saved us from a fall that most likely would have ended in our deaths if she hadn't been there. That's what happens when you travel by portal. You can't exactly plan for where it decides to spit you out.

But this. *This.* The water slices neatly and cleanly around us. Everything is a swirl of color: flashes of pink and purple bleeding into shades of green and blue. It's as though we're sailing through a watercolor painting. I feel weightless as we're rushed along. Schools of fish part for us to neatly slice through them. A pair of dolphins follow us along for a while, giggling all the way before losing interest and disappearing. I hear the echo-cries of a whale somewhere in the distance, reminding me that there are bigger and possibly more dangerous creatures in this sea world than Tullia.

Altair begins to gain momentum, heading upward just a little so that we have a better view of the landscape. The little houses are behind us, clustered around the castle, growing sparser the farther away we travel. In the direction we're headed, the water is less cerulean and more navy. I feel a drop in temperature and shiver, pressing myself against Sloan. He can't turn into a merman. Somewhere trapped between Ridge—born this way—and Nightfall—forced to be this way. I shake my head. It's only one arm. *Don't be so dramatic.* But I know that it won't stop there. How can it? Unless we leave before he completely changes. Then that's what we'll have to do. Even if I don't find the Water stone, we will leave before it's too late. Before we can't reverse what's been done. Before he's unable to return home with me. I tighten my grip around his waist. What does it take to break an Everlasting Vow? What happens if one is broken?

"There!" Sloan exclaims and I peer over his shoulder. Just past

Altair's head and slightly downward, I see it. Pieces and parts of tattered cloth, metal chunks, and decaying wood covered in lichen. Once parts of great ships that sailed the open sea, but now remnants from another world and another time lining the ocean floor. We've reached the graveyard.

CHAPTER 10

Sloan sends Altair into a nosedive and we're cutting through the current at a downward angle, heading straight for the white, sandy bottom. Sloan whispers something and Altair pulls up and back, allowing for a smooth landing. It's as if Sloan were born for this. In a way, maybe he was. I just hope that being here—around people like himself, well, like the other part of himself—won't make him want to stay. I know, I'm supposed to be willing to let him go because if I love him that's what you do, right? You let people go. But I won't. I refuse. I'm not that selfless. This isn't some kid's fairy tale. This is real life, and in real life you want your true love with you no matter what and no matter where.

I push the thought aside because, partly, it's my own paranoia. Sloan has a family back home. People who love him and need him. Besides me. We've only just arrived and our stay will be short. If we can find the stone.

Sloan slides off Altair's back then comes over to me, placing his hands around my waist and helping me down. I watch as he pats Altair on the neck, the sleeve of his t-shirt revealing his newly scale-covered arm. Will it go back to normal once we leave?

This part of the sea is different. Near the castle, there's the distinct subtle buzz of the life that surrounds it, but here it's oddly quiet.

"You need to stop worrying," he says.

"Were you in my thoughts again?" I ask. I'm about to give him a verbal lashing because he knows how much I hate it when he does that. It's an unfair advantage in the relationship.

But he just smiles and shakes his head. "I can see it on your face." He runs a finger across my forehead. "In the furrow of your brow." Then he drags that scaled finger down in between my eyes. "And here." He kisses me. "You have nothing to worry about."

I kiss him back seeking reassurance and comfort. *Don't you leave me too*, I think. Then I slowly pull away, my hands square on his chest. "Except finding the stone."

"Okay, except that." He takes my hand and leads me toward the graveyard. I guess old habits die hard, because we walk across the sand at first, its softness melting beneath the soles of my feet. As we draw nearer I try to piece together the ships, imagining the torn parts coming to life and reassembling themselves. Only I don't know how they fit together and I can't tell how many ships there should be. My best guess is a lot.

A school of tiny silver fish hurry out of a nearby porthole window, shiny bodies like coins tossed into the sea as they swim past us. The feeling here is hard to explain. It's like entering a dream that's extremely vivid, almost exquisite in its detail, only to wake up and not remember a thing. We walk to the hull of the ship and stare into the window the fish swam out of. All that peers back at us is blackness. These ships were once alive. There were people—human people— aboard these ships. And now they are all gone. Some have become Tullia's guards-lovers-slaves, but what about the others? Where have they gone? I push myself through the round window and reach into my messenger bag to pull out a flashlight. It flicks on and the beam of light sweeps over the interior wreckage.

An overturned table, silverware, chipped mugs and dishes are scattered across the ship's sandy insides. This must have been the dining area or kitchen of the ship. Sloan squeezes himself through the hole and nods his head to the left and I swim after him, the flashlight bouncing off the remains of the ship. Peeling wallpaper, shards of glass that shimmer in the light's golden beam. In all of this mess we're looking for a single opal stone. The stones are part of me, once I get close I usually feel drawn right to it, like some sort of invisible tether that connects me to it. But here, I feel like the stone could be any of the millions of seashells that line the sea floor.

Sloan leads me to a flight of stairs and we float up them, our feet never touching the ground. We round a corner and are greeted by a door with a round window in it. The lichen-covered glass is still intact. Sloan edges open the door and leaves enough space for us to slip through. I swing the flashlight around the room. There's a large wooden wheel with spokes in it. I've never seen anything like it. Granted, I haven't been on many—okay, any—boats in my lifetime on Xon 9.

"This is the bridge," Sloan says. His voice melodious in the silence.

"It doesn't look like a bridge."

He grins. "That's what this room is called. It's where the captain steers the ship. This is the steering wheel." He swims up to it, placing a hand on either side. One dark green-gray hand, one lightly bronzed hand. I swim around the room, examining the instruments that helped the captain steer this vessel, my curiosity getting the better of me and for a moment forgetting about the Water stone. These ships are pieces from a time when I possibly didn't even exist. When no one on Xon 9 existed. It's like time has stopped and is trapped, here on the bottom of the sea, while the rest of the world continued above. When the sun that gave Old Earth its life burned itself up and died, as all stars eventually do—these ships stayed here—wherever here is exactly. It's hard to say when dealing with other lands and portals, but this place feels eerily…Old Earth-like. Before the scientists found Xon 9 and started a colony. Before the end of the world and a new one began. Now, maybe just a little, I understand why Sloan loves history so much.

The beam of my flashlight falls on something that glitters. Once I'm closer, I realize it's a gold picture frame. In the frame is a photo of a man and a woman. The woman is beautiful with short, brown hair that makes her large eyes and high cheekbones stand out. She is wearing a long skirt and a simple tank top. Her arm is around the man's waist and the man has very short black hair. He's lean and fit, wearing a button down white shirt and khaki shorts. They're standing on a beach: white sand, blue sea, palm trees. There's no place like that in the Universe. At least not anymore. At least not that I know of. I inspect the image closer and my heart tightens in my chest. The angular jawline and the deep-set eyes. If the hair was grown out long and to his shoulders and he happened to be holding a trident, I'd recognize that face. It's Nightfall.

Tullia did this. The woman in this picture—it could be Nightfall's wife. His human wife, who had no idea that her husband was still alive here, trapped at the bottom of the sea. What if they had kids? What were they told? I swim to the front of the bridge where there's a smashed out wall of glass, some shards still jutting out from the frame. Looking out, I can see the remnants of ships for what seems like miles. Broken vessels left to rot on the ocean floor. And for what? So Tullia could have herself a human male conquest? The image of the forked black tongue and the blood-like drink at dinner blur my vision. How could I possibly be related to this monster? Because that's what she is. Goddess or not. Family or not. She is a monster.

For reasons I can't explain, I swim back to where the picture sits on the ledge, still somehow intact despite its crumbling surroundings. With a shaking hand, I pluck it from its spot and place it inside my messenger bag. A reminder of who Nightfall is, who I am. And who

Sloan is. Tullia can use all the enchantments that she wants, but there are some things that can't be taken away. Just like the Imminent Darkness. We can be manipulated, enslaved, tortured or cursed, forced to choose, but at our very core humanness still remains.

Metal, Fire, Wood, Earth, or Water on the outside, but on the inside are blood all runs red. That's why there never really was a choice to be made. I am part of it. Working to collect all the pieces of who I am. And now Li is part of it too, but for the exact opposite reasons. I am all and he is none. And yet we are the same. Human beings. With very real human feelings. That's something the Imminent Darkness could never understand. But it's something my mother *did* understand, and was willing to risk the entire Universe for, and it's why Nightfall told me where to look for the stone. It's why Sloan is with me now even as his physical body begins to change in ways that he has no control over. And it's the reason I take the photograph with me.

Simple, stupid, irrational. Complicated, infinite, magical. Really, it's the only reason there ever was, is or will be. Love.

. . .

We spend more time turning over seashells then finding anything worthwhile. How are we ever going to find the opal stone? Usually, the stone's location isn't discreet, and I'd have to agree with Nightfall that the graveyard seems as good as a place as any. But did he truly send me here to find the stone, or to find something more?

Eventually, I insist that we split up. What's the point in both of us searching the same ship? We could cover more ground if we searched separately. And the sooner we find the stone, the sooner we can return home. Before Sloan's entire body turns into a merman and he can no longer physically return home. Because that appears to be a very real possibility. My mother could have mentioned that bit before we left. Reluctantly, Sloan agrees.

I'm swimming through the remains of the next ship. Sloan has gone down to the other end, or what I assume is the end of the graveyard and then he will continue at the opposite end until we meet somewhere in the middle. Altair stayed with me. That was the only way I could convince Sloan to split up. The waterdragon is outside the shipwreck, keeping watch. But more than likely, he's taking a nap or watching the schools of fish swim by. The word dragon seems a bit of a misnomer since he seems to be more docile than dangerous.

My flashlight sweeps through the narrow hallway. This ship is not as fancy as the previous one. There's no wallpaper or silver dinnerware. Everything is rotted wood and tin cans. The water is colder and darker here. I'm in what would be the bottom of the ship. I see chains coiled up, taken over by lichen. More of those tiny silver fish swim through a porthole to my left and then exit through one on the opposite wall. The ship's remains lean toward the right and it has a disorienting affect.

All of the other stones were protected in some way. The Fire stone was kept in the base of a volcano; the Earth stone was kept safe in a strange pyramid with booby traps throughout; and the Wood stone was located in an abandoned amber mine, and protected by a beast that could project back to you your weakness, thus making it even harder to kill and retrieve the stone. Even still, it wasn't the beast's fault any more than it was the volcano's fault. I reach the front end of the ship and there's nowhere to go but back the way I came. Except before I turn around, I notice a hole in the floor above my head. That floor would have been the main deck of the ship.

I swim through the narrow hole and my bag snags on its jagged edges, jerking me backward. I yank it free, careful not to spill its contents. This ship has been broken in half. In between the halves are the remains of what Sloan told me is called a mast. At one time it had cloth sails that could be used to direct its course of travel. We may have out-of-use transportation portals, cloaking cuffs, and holographic devices back home, but I find the fact that some pieces of fabric could take you any direction in the world to be pretty amazing. I swim over to the bow of the ship. Some of its railing is still intact and I follow it along until I reach the figurehead.

The figurehead is carved of wood and it immediately reminds me of the *Gallery of Tullia*. It's a mermaid with hair floating above her head like a crown. Her tale is curved and from the hipbones upward, she has the body of woman, except there is a carved seashell over either breast. I appreciate the artist's discretion. The mermaid's eyes are open and her mouth is in a smile. No, not a smile. A snarl, revealing sharp pointed teeth. This is no ordinary mermaid. Perhaps it is the siren my mother spoke of. I run my finger along its face, tracing the craftsmanship, when my finger feels a small hole, right between the siren's eyes. I lean in closer shining the flashlight across her face, blank wood eyes staring back at me. A rainbow shines in the beam of the flashlight. Turquoise, chartreuse, cobalt, fuchsia, lavender, tangerine…any color you can think of is contained in the tiny space between her eyes. How did it get there? I stick my finger in deeper, trying to dig at the rainbow and my finger finds something cool and smooth. Like a tiny stone! Maybe the Water stone. Somehow though I imagined it would be a bit bigger.

I reach into my bag and pull out a small, jewel encrusted dagger. Really, it is Sloan's and not mine. A gift from Qildor, the Keeper of the Genesis. I take the sharp point of the blade and dig it into the siren's forehead. Let's be honest, she's probably seen better days. Shards of wood peel away like paper, floating to the sand below. But the stone hasn't budged, despite my handiwork at giving the siren a third eye. So, I decide that I need a different tactic. I wedge the tip of the blade into the hole, then saying a silent prayer that I don't break Sloan's gift from the friend we'll probably never see again and who helped save both of our lives, I give the handle a solid *thwack!*

And the opal stone comes flying out in a perfect arc over my head before sinking to the sand behind me. That mostly worked. Perhaps my trajectory was a bit off. Unfortunately, the siren now has a gaping hole in her head. Fortunately, I may have found the Water stone. I swim down to the sand about where the stone landed.

I'm searching for rainbows. There are a few pieces of broken shell, but after glimpsing what I think is the actual stone, the opalescence doesn't even compare. The seashells are merely shiny in comparison, casting dull rainbows on their flat surfaces. This stone looked like a living rainbow was contained within itself, curving and spiraling, the colors so vibrant it was as if they were glowing against the smooth, white surface.

A little flicker, like a flame in the sand. *Gotcha.* I reach down scooping the small stone up, turning it in between my webbed fingers, and admiring it. It's too bad the next part of what I have to do is destroy it. Find the stones, retrieve them, and then destroy them. Then and only then would that missing piece of the puzzle that is Ka be returned to me.

Water is nurturing, serene, and fluid. But, as Sloan is always quick to remind me, that which sustains us can also kill us. That's a lot of power to give to any one element. Unbalanced Water is unpredictable and tumultuous. One minute calm as a bubbling brook, and the next a raging tsunami.

Once Sloan took the time to explain to me about some of the natural disasters on Old Earth: floods, tidal waves, tsunamis, monsoons, hurricanes…so many disasters caused by water, given the conduciveness of numerous other conditions, of course. And then there's water's opposite, its balance: drought. Not enough water. No water equals no life. The planet, like the Universe, was always maintaining itself in a perfect, perpetual balance. A flood on one side of the world and a drought on the other. Too much in one, not enough in the other.

He then went on to explain to me one of the reasons he was drawn to Water. He said that despite the floods and tidal waves—all the big stuff—being destructive, the paradox of water is that the tiniest of trickles can have just as much of an impact. There was a book that he'd shown me, a very old book with many geographical features of Old Earth contained within it. He showed me a picture of something called the Grand Canyon. An entire canyon carved by a single river over millions of years. Patient and persistent. That is why he chose Water.

The duality of Water is what scared me because I didn't know which side I'd end up on, as I stood in that black box at Pronouncement. *Personality Strengths: above average intellect, highly observant, and extremely loyal. Personality Weaknesses: stubbornness, indecisiveness, and the inability to speak one's mind. Calculating recommendation. Recommendation: Water.* The automated female voice comes back to me as if it just happened yesterday. Despite the recommendation, you could still choose. That right had been granted to us. Either way though, you had to make a choice. And I chose Fire. I said I was scared of *him*. Not knowing the full story, I thought that I didn't want to be where he was, when in actuality deep down I wanted to be anywhere and everywhere that he was. That was my predicament. I didn't trust myself enough to make the right decision. And that scared me, because our Council of Leaders may all be Woods and Metals may be our soldiers, but Water is the life force. They are nurturers, those who give life, but they can take it all away. And, truly, no one should have that kind of power. Look at Tullia.

I tuck the small stone into my pocket and toss my flashlight back into my messenger bag. It's time to wake up Altair and go find Sloan to tell him that I've found the Water stone. It's time to go home. I'm almost disappointed. No volcanoes erupted on me. No living dead mummy chased me. And no beast tried to eat me and then leave my bones in a nauseating heap with its other helpless victims. I turn to go retrieve Altair and my stomach drops. I think I spoke too soon.

CHAPTER 11

A bulbous, white eye stares back at me. Except, it's as big as my entire face. I stumble backwards over the sand. My brain tries to compute exactly what it is that I am seeing. The creature is leaning over, as if inspecting me. Even still, its body towers over me. Its charcoal colored body is slimy and squishy looking. There's no visible mouth, no nose, no gills, no fins. My brain recognizes it from Old Earth biology textbooks, but my words can't formulate the word for it. I notice the tentacles too late. One reaches out and begins to curl around my waist, squeezing as if it wants to juice the life out of me. Octopus? That would have been helpful to remember a couple of seconds ago.

The tentacles are ridiculously long and wind around my waist multiple times. It lifts me as it rights itself and I'm soaring through the sea. The shipwrecks become little dots below me. I'm still clutching Sloan's dagger in my hand, but with my arms bound to either side it's pretty much useless. How does something this large live in the sea? I do the math pretty quickly. All of the shipwrecks. Tullia's insatiable desire. This beast is her pet. It captures the ships and pulls them down into the ocean's depths. But what is it? No Old Earth octopus was this gigantic.

Other tentacles, as round as several men, and as long as a tree is tall, wave around in the water around us, creating a strong current. I yell out for Sloan, but when I do the tentacle binding me just grows tighter. Its eyes dart around in its ginormous head, reminding me of a doll I had as a child. The doll's eyes opened and closed, and sometimes they sort of rolled around aimlessly in its plastic head. That's how this monster looks. The water here is deeper and darker than near the castle. I wonder if it can even see in the light of day. It takes me away from the shipwrecks—and Sloan's location. Growing smaller with each burst forward. It's like floating through the sea. While having the life almost squeezed out of you. If only I could use the dagger. I'm pretty sure I wouldn't be able to kill it. Might not even harm it, given the size of the dagger and the size of the beast. But maybe I could startle it at least.

I try to sort through my options. Fire. Electricity. Yeah, but we're in water. What happens to me when that happens? I'm not sure and I don't think that I want to find out. Wood. Do I really need to know the span of this guy's life? Not really. That leaves Earth. Vines. That could work. All I need to do is think it to summon them. In immediate answer I feel the pulsation on the inside of my wrists, where my veins run green instead of blue around the almost imperceptible incision marks. I haven't quite mastered full control of this ability yet, but my current options are limited. The vines shoot out of my wrists as if they have a mind of their own and begin wrapping themselves around the part of the tentacle not tightly wound around my body. They're like thick, green ropes that will continue to rush out until I will them to stop. I watch as they wrap tighter and tighter, like some kind of plant boa constrictor. Unfortunately, as this happens, I feel my grip on the dagger loosen and float away into the sea of nothingness beneath me.

Once I see the tentacle growing pale around me, I snap off the vines. The monster peers at me, all google-eyed. Suddenly, it seems to dawn on him what is happening and the other tentacles wave around angrily. This was not thoroughly thought-out. As the circulation of the tentacle is cut off, I can feel myself slipping away. Except there are about twenty other tentacles that can grab me. And that's exactly what happens. I begin to slip out of the beast's grasp and as I slide out I can take a gulp of air. Even with gills, it feels good to breathe, if only for a second because another giant tentacle is swiping at me. It winds around my legs, smashing them together and I can feel the sensation of bone crunching.

I'm pulled upward by my legs, all the blood rushing to my head in a throbbing crescendo. It dangles me in front of its face. Tentacles part and for the first time I see a large mouth. Full of long, pointy teeth roughly the same size as my entire body. I have no choice. I just hope it doesn't hurt me as much as I hope to hurt it. I close my eyes and will my Fire to the surface. Anger. Anger at Tullia for what she's done to so many innocent men. Anger at the Imminent Darkness for wrecking my colony. Anger at myself for not being able to stop it before someone else gets hurt or worse. The anger boils to the surface easily, a silent rage that has been coursing through me for far too long with nowhere to go. No one else on Xon 9 is like me. No one else carries this burden. How could anyone else possibly understand?

I feel the warmth turning hot inside me. Fire is passion. Fire is anger. Like water, fire can be both a giver and taker of life. The current bursts out of me, out of every cell and through every pore. The smell of burning flesh mixing with the saltiness of the sea. The tentacle's grip loosens and once again I feel myself slipping away, drifting downward. The current around me has stopped and I shake and convulse as I swirl down to the ocean floor. Water and electricity don't mix. Half-immortal. But only half. It takes me a second to realize that the smell of burning flesh was mine. My eyes slide closed as I hit the sea's sandy bottom.

...

Strong arms pick me up, an arm placed carefully beneath my head and another under my knees. Instinctively, I wrap my arms around the neck of my rescuer. I'm alive. I think. Well, I'm pretty sure. I feel myself floating through the sea smoothly. Someone who's done this before. Even in my semi-consciousness, my heart sinks. Not Sloan. Sloan can swim, sure. But he's still human. Mostly. We come to a stop and I'm laid onto a hard surface. Someone is shaking my shoulder. A tether in the blackness that surrounds me. He can't call my name because he doesn't know it.

I open my eyes and through the fuzziness I can see two human eyes looking back at me. They're the color of stars, a luminescent hazel color that seem to glow. Down here, who knows, maybe they do. No nose, but a gill in either cheek. Silver-white scales line the side of the face peering back at me and I will my eyes to focus, so that I can properly see my rescuer. The face leans over me, peering closely. I feel a small hand resting gently over my heart, checking my breathing. A long, red tendril of hair falls across my cheek.

My rescuer is not a he, but a she.

Chapter 12

Her name is Cerise. She sits across from me, her long pearlescent tail wrapped beneath her. Her skin is porcelain white. Her scales stop just above where her belly button would be and her long, red hair covers up her chest almost in some weird magical way, as if it is both her hair and her clothing.

"Thank you," I say for the umpteenth time.

"The kraken is a horrible creature," she replies. Her mouth is bright pink and I bet that there is not a forked-black tongue hiding in there. Cerise is mesmerizingly beautiful. More beautiful than I thought Tullia was before I met her. But her beauty seems fragile, not fierce. And yet, I know that she is as strong as any man if she was able to pick up my body's deadweight and carry me to safety.

We sit on top of a stone ledge that looks out over the sea below. The water is clearer here, golden light shining down from above.

There is rainbow-colored coral beneath us and a school of tiny fish swim past. I don't know where we are, or where Sloan is. I'm a stranger in a strange land. Even stranger is being a human in a land where there are none.

"A kraken? Is that what that giant octopus thing is called?"

Cerise laughs and it sounds as if the heavens of the old religion have opened and is what I imagine the angels would sound like. It's almost painful to my human senses that Cerise is so beautiful looking and beautiful sounding. So far she also seems genuinely nice, as if being and sounding ethereal weren't enough. "You're funny, human girl."

"Ka. My name's Ka," I correct.

"That's a peculiar name." But she's smiling when she says it.

"It means Fire." I reply with a shrug. "Cerise is a weird name too." I point out just to be fair. She looks to be around my age. But it's hard to tell with these mermaid types. For all I know she could be three-hundred-and-ninety-two.

She sighs and pulls a strand of long red hair between her index and middle fingers, as if she were going to snip it off. "It means cherry."

I laugh. "That wasn't very nice."

She laughs too. "It's better than Ginger or Red, I suppose. But not by much." A silence falls between us, but it feels comfortable, as if we are old friends.

"Why did you save me?" I ask.

"You were dying." She gestures. "And injured."

I inspect my left hand. My middle, ring, and pinky fingers have all been charred black. Luckily, my turquoise ring is still secure on my index finger. I wish I could say the same for Sloan's dagger. "Eh. I'm half-immortal," I reply.

"Only half. That means the other half can still die."

"Thanks, but I was, you know, trying to be an optimist."

Her brow furrows. "I don't know this word."

I sigh. "That's okay. It just means, looking for the best in things." I curl and uncurl my blackened fingers.

She nods, understanding flooding those mysterious eyes. She seems so familiar to me, I could swear that I've seen her before. I just can't place where. Or when.

"That I understand." She pauses as if debating whether or not to say something more, then finally she asks, "Were you out in the sea all alone? Did your boat capsize?"

"Huh? Oh. No. I don't have a boat. I had a water dragon, but he's probably gone by now. I'm staying with my Aunt Tullia."

"Your aunt is the Water Queen?" Cerise's face gets a pinched expression and I can immediately tell that she is not as big a fan of Tullia as Tullia is of Tullia.

"Unfortunately. That's where the half-immortal part comes from." I flex and unflex my fingers. The webbing has torn away. If I wasn't watching myself do it, I wouldn't feel a thing. "I'm kind of on a mission of sorts. I was looking for something."

"Did you find it?" Her face is curious and her eyes are sincere.

"I did. Except, in the process I seem to have lost my boyfriend."

"Oh, that's horrible!" she blushes. "I've never had a proper boyfriend."

I look at her perfect little, heart-shaped face. "Are you kidding me? You're gorgeous. And obviously kind. The guys here must be confused."

She giggles. "Mermen aren't really my type." She lowers her voice as if we could be heard up here in the seemingly middle of nowhere. "They tend to be on the conceited side."

"Somehow that doesn't surprise me."

"How will you find your boyfriend?" She runs a finger back and forth along the stone between us, making a five-pointed-star pattern over and over again.

"I don't know."

"Where did you last see him? Before the kraken took you?" Her face cloud's over at the mention of the monster. I wonder what other personal experiences she's had with it, or if she's simply forever cleaning up its leftovers.

"At the ship graveyard."

"That's an interesting place." She moves a bit of hair and shows me a dainty, silver necklace with an arrow charm on it. "I found this there once."

"It's very pretty. Do you go there a lot?"

"Only when I'm bored."

"And how often is that?"

"Every day. That's where I was headed when I found you. The kraken doesn't particularly like the light. That's why I brought you up here."

"Would you want to go back with me? And help me find Sloan? That's my boyfriend." I don't know why I'm asking her. Even though she seems nice, for all I know she could be a crazy, ravenous siren who wants to eat me. You just never can be too sure.

"Yes, Ka-whose-name-means-Fire, I will go with you and help you to find your Sloan."

Her eyes are lit up, glowing from within and her skin is radiant, like the Water stone itself. I never would have imagined that I'd befriend a mermaid. I wonder why this perfect-looking creature saved me, when she could have just left me to die. But here she is and here we are. That's when I recognize the glow in her eyes because I realize I've seen it before. It's the same glow in Li's eyes right before something exciting is about to happen. Adventure. I guess it isn't every day you find a human in a sea world, just lying in your front yard. It's about as strange as my befriending a mermaid. Once again, as Sloan always tells me, stranger things have happened.

CHAPTER 13

Turns out the Kraken took me pretty far from the graveyard. Naturally, Cerise is an elegant, fast swimmer. Unlike myself. I'm much more tired than I'd like to admit. Half-immortal or not, I think I may have a cracked rib. Eventually, Cerise insists that I wrap my arms around her neck and let her carry me. The girl's not kidding. Her looks may be ethereal, but her physical strength is just as out of this world.

Ignoring my protests, she wraps my arms over her shoulders, forcing me to clasp my hands in front just under her pointy chin. I rest my own chin on her slender shoulder. Up close her skin is even more shimmery, like she's made out of crushed pearls. Her silky red hair rubs against my cheek and she smells like peaches and saltwater. It's a strange combination because I'm pretty sure there are no peach trees down here.

We swim swiftly without speaking and I feel like time is a weight strung heavily around my neck. Even though I'm still not sure how the passage of time is marked down here. Time in the lands passes differently than on Xon 9, but with no sun or moon there's nothing to mark the hours. After a while, I can see the remnants of the ship yard coming into view. There's no sign of Altair which most likely means there's no Sloan either. My stomach sinks.

"It doesn't look like anyone is here," Cerise says over her shoulder.

"No. It doesn't." It's hard to hide the dejection from my voice. "He must have thought I went back to the castle."

"I will take you there." Without my consent, she swims upward, sailing over the grave yard of ships that sail no more. I'm too tired to protest.

But what will Tullia think of Cerise? She's certainly younger looking and much more beautiful. And so far definitely kinder. Surely, Tullia will see her as a threat. But what will Cerise think of Tullia? Clearly, she has disdain for the Water Queen and possibly her insatiable desires for consuming earthly men. This has the potential to get interesting. Or dangerous.

The golden glow of the castle comes into view. If Tullia can swim as fast as Cerise, then Altair must just be another one of her many toys to show off. Cerise pulls up as we near the castle, slowly drifting us downward. I can feel the muscles tense in her shoulders. Several yards away from the castle, I carefully disentangle myself from Cerise's back.

"You don't have to come with me. You don't seem like the biggest fan of the Water Queen." I smile, "Actually, I'm pretty sure that I don't like her either."

Cerise smiles back, but it doesn't meet her eyes this time. She glances over my shoulder toward the castle. "I'll be close."

"How will I be able to find you?" It seems stupid to even ask. Sloan and I are leaving. I found the Water stone, so now it's time to get the hell out of town.

She leans in and presses her lips to my ear and makes a long, low trill from deep within her throat. "Just do that."

"Um, sure." I have no idea how she'd be able to hear that from anywhere in the sea. Maybe mermaids have supersonic hearing in addition to superhuman strength. I hug her. "Thanks for saving me."

Her eyes cloud over. "It won't be the last time." She turns, her hair covering her face, so that I can't see her expression. I blink and in that amount of time all I see is a glimmering white tail fin in the distance. If today hasn't been one of the weirdest days of my life.

I watch until I can't see Cerise anymore, which takes all of one more second, then turn back and head toward the castle. As I near the drawbridge, Nightfall stands patiently, holding his trident, face stony. When he notices me I see a slight change, a softening in his features.

"Hi."

"You don't look too good," he replies, his eyes darting to my left hand.

"You shouldn't say that to a woman. It could have catastrophic consequences. Especially around here." I reach into my messenger bag and finger the gilded frame. Before I can lose the courage, I pull out the picture of George and the woman, thrusting it at him. "I found this. Thought you might want it."

I stare at my blackened fingers, as if inspecting them. After a few moments of silence, I steal a glance at Nightfall's face. "I'm sorry," I whisper, unsure if I've done more harm than good.

A single tear rolls down his scaled face before hitting his chin and floating away, sucked up into the sea. "Her name was Helene."

"You look happy."

"The happiest." He presses the frame to his chest as if he could physically push it into his body and merge it with his heart space. "Did you find what you were looking for?"

"I did." I take in this muscular man, with his tattooed enchantment, seemingly so intimidating, but in this moment, looking broken. "And more."

"Your Water man. He's here. He thought you'd returned when he wasn't able to find you." There's a weird tone to Nightfall's voice as if he wants to say more. He hesitates, then looks down at the photograph. "Your boyfriend. He looked different when he came back."

My heart begins to thump double time in my chest. "How so?"

Nightfall takes his hand holding the trident and gestures at his own body. "It's happening to him."

"Where we're from, he's a Water Elemental. It was only a matter of time before he adapted to this environment," I explain. And yet somehow I know it could never be that simple. If it was, then why wasn't I able to adapt to the heat and raining plasma in the Land of Fire? Why can I not anamorph like my mother in the Land of Earth?

"I wish it were that simple, Princess." I've been called Princess before. By Li as a joke when I found out who I truly am and just what my lineage meant., and by my friend Brooks who lived in the enchanted lake in the Elemental Abyss and who was killed by the Imminent Darkness. Killed in cold blood. I realize an understanding of some sort—an exchange of trust—has just occurred between Nightfall and me. "She can't be trusted."

He looks back down at the photograph. Of smiling faces. Of another man in another world, possibly even in another lifetime. "You deserve to know the truth, so I will tell you."

When he looks back up his eyes are resolute, but I still feel sick to my stomach. "Tullia is a wicked woman who entraps men with her kraken. At first, a man tries his best to fight it. Using all of his physical and mental strength to resist. But the water, it's a good conductor for carrying an enchantment." I think of Sloan as he kissed me beneath the tapestry of Tullia, the desire and need that belied it. His dilated pupils and his fragmented breath. The feeling that something was different here. "Once, the enchantment has taken effect, it's useless. There's no way to fight it and once you...well, once Tullia has her way with you...that's how the curse is embedded. It's a curse that courses through my own blood and entraps me here." He gestures to his curled tail. "How would I ever go home like this? And if I had made it home how would I ever have explained it to Helene?" His voice falls flat, but I don't have the time to console him right now.

Because realization dawns on me. Ridge's adoring eyes. The human men who were turned into statues and the mermen with their mysterious, glowing, rearranging tattoos. All of these souls were Tullia's sexual conquests. Her enchantment strengthened by the natural currents endlessly moving through this water world. Men unable to control their desire and lust for the Water Queen, and ever a loving queen, she would indulge their desires and in the process entrap them here. Forever. I only hope that I'm not too late.

CHAPTER 14

The castle is huge and I don't know where Tullia's bedroom is, but my instincts tell me the top most floor. I hurry down the hallway past where our bedrooms were until I reach the end where there is another spiraling staircase. I follow it. My heart pounds in my chest. I could call for Cerise. But then the element of surprise would be gone. I reach the top of the steps and come face to face with a closed door, its white opalescence contradictory to the debauchery it contains within. I close my eyes and take a deep breath. And push open the door. The fact that it wasn't locked, doesn't surprise me. Tullia wanted this. Wanted me to know. Probably since she saw Sloan's face hovering over that basin of water in my mother's kitchen.

The scene that greets me is as expected, but it doesn't make it any easier to digest. Sloan is on his back in an opulent bed made of glistening seashells and gauzy white curtains that are pulled back just enough to reveal the bed's contents. His face turns at my entrance, and even from here I can see that his normally green eyes are completely black. I've been the victim of an enchantment once, and he helped to save me. Now, it's time to return the favor. It's me saving him for once.

My stomach turns and bile rises at the sight of Tullia astride *my* boyfriend. *My* protector. Sloan. Somehow she has grown two human legs and I realize with a sinking feeling that I'm dealing with a person and a magic much more complex than I'd originally thought. Her human legs still have silvery scales and her hands are on either side of Sloan's shoulders, her chest pressed against his, her blue-tipped hair spilling across the bed.

I'm dizzy. I want to throw up. I try to focus. Even from here I can see that Sloan's arm is completely covered in silvery-green scales that have now spread across his chest and stomach. Tullia's body blocks his waist, but I can see his jeans are still on. Maybe Sloan hasn't been cursed. Yet. Or maybe I'm too late and this is just the after deed snuggle fest.

Tullia turns to me, lavender eyes flecked with menace. Not wavering she leans over, her eyes still on me, and uses her forked black-tongue to lick Sloan's cheek. I see his chest rise and fall, and hear the audible sigh as his hands roam her hips. She wants me to cry. She's expecting me to run away and leave him here. Like hell.

I cross the room in two strides and swing my messenger bag in an arc that clocks her across the face and knocks her off her throne. Some things just aren't made for sharing. I bound over to Sloan's body, his black eyes looking at me but not registering who I am. Tullia is getting up, eyes blazing. I'm about to clock her again, when she blocks it with a thin arm. The bag is thrust away, practically taking me with it. So the super strength isn't unique to Cerise. But that's okay, because I don't need super strength. I am pissed off. And sometimes that's enough.

I lean over and hurl myself into her slender waist. She's so shocked that she has no time to brace for the impact. I'm on top of her now and I won't stop hitting her precious, perfect siren face that hides such an ugly, despicable, murderer beneath it. She doesn't bleed. I didn't expect her to.

She growls and bucks her hips trying to throw me off, but I refuse to budge. I was born with my legs and that's my advantage. Adrenaline surges through me and allowing my strength to rival her own. I squeeze my knees into her sides and she winces. Nightfall's life. Gone. A wife, maybe even kids. Never able to see their dad again. All those statues downstairs. The other guards with the tattooed curse, a constant reminder of what they've lost.

"How many?" I find myself screaming, shaking her against the stone floor. "How many, Tullia? Hundreds? Thousands?"

I can feel the surge continuing inside me, but I'm helpless to control it. She gave them no choice, and truly that's what this whole thing is about. What it's been about all this time. Choice. I feel the sparks inside me, leaking from my pores and I know what's about to happen, but it's gone too far. I can't stop it. What happens when you're immortal gifts are used on another immortal? We're about to find out. The surge is so strong that I'm flung backwards. Golden sparks fly out of my body and Tullia screams, a horrible high-pitched wail. Immortal doesn't mean that you can't be hurt. Can't become damaged. It just means that you live forever. Live forever with the consequences of what you've done.

The sparks don't stop. They stream out of me and wrap themselves up in a cocoon around Tullia as if they are a living and breathing thing themselves, first binding her legs together, then continuing up her body. "Ka! You wouldn't do this to your aunt! Would you? I'm family! I was only having a little fun!"

I put my hands over my ears. "SHUT. UP."

The sparks are up to her shoulders now. A glowing cocoon. How long will it keep her there? I don't know. What will it do to her? I'm not sure I care.

"Kat—" Her words are swallowed up by the golden threads of electricity. They pulsate like a shining star. I don't wait to find out what happens next.

I grab Sloan's black t-shirt from the floor and toss it to him. "Get dressed. We're going home."

He catches the shirt one-handed. Sitting up, I can see that his entire stomach and above his waistband are covered in scales. One arm is and one arm isn't. Without looking I somehow know that his legs are probably covered too. He regards me with unblinking, black eyes. He doesn't move.

This isn't going as planned.

I grab his wrist and yank him behind me, moving easily out of the building before Ridge or anyone finds Tullia and tries to make me pay for what I've done. Past the statues, except I notice that something is different. The statues aren't the same. Something crunches beneath my foot. They're crumbling. There's an arm there and a chunk of someone's face over there. When I look more closely I can see that there are fissures in the stone. Sloan doesn't resist as I pull him along. This is the quietest he's ever been and I wonder if that's part of the enchantment, or if he just doesn't know what to say. Because if it's the latter, he's not the only one.

We emerge from the castle and no one is there. No Ridge. No Nightfall. No schools of fish swimming by. Something in the water has changed. I can feel it. Sloan pulls at my arm and I turn to see him on his knees, head bowed over. I kneel beside him and place a hand behind his neck, carefully lowering him so that his upper body rests across my knees and the rest of his body across the sandy floor. I see bits of emerald green appearing at the outer corners of where his irises should be. And right then I know that he sees me, *really* sees me, and knows that I came to save him.

He makes a muffled noise, but I can't make out the words. I hold onto him, frozen with the sense that something horrible is about to happen. He begins to convulse in my arms, eyes rolled back in his head. Bits of pale green foam form at the corners of his mouth and my heart seizes in my chest. I can't think. Don't know what's happening. Don't know what to do. I'm all alone. So, I do the only thing that I can remember in that moment of sheer panic. I throw back my head and let out a long, trilling sound.

The water current picks it up, acting like an amplifier. The note ends, swallowed up by the sea and I look down at Sloan in my arms. His eyes unseeing, his body still convulsing. This isn't how it's supposed to be. He's the one who's supposed to protect *me*. Save *me*. I only hope that Cerise isn't too late.

. . .

One moment Cerise isn't there. And then suddenly she is. As if appearing out of thin air. But there's no time to question. Her discerning hazel eyes take in Sloan's seizing form and my panicked expression. She rushes over and brushes the hair back from his face as if she's inspecting it.

"What happened?"

"Tullia."

"Of course." She doesn't ask anything more. We're running out of time. I can feel his pulse slowing beneath my fingertips. "It's the enchantment or the curse. I'm not sure which," she says.

"I don't think it's the curse. I don't think they…you know."

Her eyes darken. "I know." She runs her fingers over Sloan's neck. "We don't have much time. But it's good he hasn't completely turned." She says noticing his very human legs. "We need to get away from here. Further away. The enchantment is stronger the closer we are to her." She begins to pick Sloan up, but I put out a hand to stop her. I put my fingers in my mouth and whistle, hoping that Altair will hear it and somehow that he'll know it's me. I'm not disappointed. He struck me as a bright beast and that's exactly what he is. Not everyone is as loyal to her as Tullia may think. Or want.

"Cerise. Altair. Altair. Cerise. Let's go." She scoops Sloan up in her arms and I help pull them both up behind me and onto Altair's back. I grip his ridged main and whisper in his ear. "As far away as you can go."

He's off like a shot. We burst through the magenta sea grass. Soaring upward. He's two—no three—times as fast as Cerise. We're gliding through the water like a bullet. I look below and the castle is becoming a small dot behind us. I wonder what happened to Nightfall. Did I injure him too when I entrapped Tullia? I'm pretty sure she's still alive.

"It's working!" Cerise says from behind me. "The seizures have stopped and his eyes are closed."

"Just a little further," I say half to myself and half to my companions.

Altair continues to swim. The water around us grows lighter and there are underwater mountains with nooks and crannies, out of which schools of rainbow colored fish dart in and out. The rainbow coral has changed to a pristine white. The stones and rocks are purple. Green and orange seagrasses sway in the current.

"Over there!" Cerise points. I guide Altair to a rocky outcropping that flattens at its summit. We are so high up that I can see the sun— or something like it—shining through the water above us. I slide off Altair and take Sloan from Cerise's arms. He's deadweight. *But not dead*, I remind myself. I lay him down gently. Altair looks at me curiously and then when I don't give him any more directives, he lays himself down and curls into a ball, tail up around his giant nose, eyes worried. I kneel beside Sloan, pressing my fingers to his neck, holding my own breath until I feel the slow, rhythmic beat beneath my fingertips.

I can't hold back the tears any longer. First, Nightfall. Then the kraken. And as if that weren't enough, to return to see my aunt seducing my boyfriend. Not only seducing him, but fully-prepared to curse him. A life without Sloan is something my brain can't compute. My tears fall, but as soon as they slide off my chin they float upward. Bina saw this. Cerise reaches out and catches my tears on her finger, holding her finger up to her face, like she's inspecting them.

"I've never seen human tears before," she says, her tiny mouth puckered thoughtfully.

But my mind is spinning. Bina saw it.

"Bina saw it!" I say out loud.

Cerise looks up confsued. "Who's Bina?"

I throw my arms around her, tears of sadness quickly turning into tears of hope. *Even if it could save the one you love?* I pull my messenger bag around and lift the flap, feeling around in its contents and inside the burlap sack, until I find the torn piece of paper.

"This!" I declare unable to hide my smile.

"A yellowed-piece of paper?" Cerise asks, clearly still confused. I can't really blame her when she's only getting about half the story.

"Sloan's mother can see the future. She gave me this and told me it could save the one I love." The future has become the present. I unfold the piece of paper.

CHAPTER 15

My heart sinks and tears burn at the backs of my eyes. I can't read it. It's in some weird language of symbols and letters, and it's unrecognizable. Useless. So much for that idea. I toss the paper aside angrily and it floats over to Cerise, who picks it up gingerly.

"Oh," she says her eyes scanning. "Oh, my. This is the ancient sea language."

I feel the hope slice like a dagger through me, cutting clear to my heart. "You know it?"

"All sea creatures do. At least the ones who pay attention."

"What does it say?"

"It appears to be an enchantment." She bites her lip. "It's a dark enchantment. But…"

"But?"

"It's very dangerous." She looks up at me. "And you're already injured."

"Oh, it's nothing. I feel fine." I flip my hand with the blackened three fingers dismissively, only it's no longer only three fingers. The black skin runs all the way up to my elbow. The electricity binding Tullia. A small sacrifice to make.

Cerise reaches over Sloan's body and takes my hand. "I will do it, Friend."

"You've already helped me more than once, Cerise."

"Is that not what friends do?"

"Yes, but…"

"But?" she asks mimicking my tone from earlier. She pauses, still holding my hand, grasping my fingers tightly. "I will help on one condition."

My heart pounds in my chest, crashing against my ribs. Here it is again. It's only fair. I can't always do the taking, at some point I also need to do the giving. "Name it." My voice comes out sounding much more self-assured than I feel. I feel like my insides are slowly beginning to crumble.

Her words come out in a tumbled rush. "Take me with you." She's pressing the piece of paper to her heart. Her hazel eyes are lit with fire. *Fire.* Now, I know why she looks familiar. She's the girl from my vision. The girl I saw with Li, except in that vision she was clearly human. Maybe the visions aren't prefect. Then again, maybe they are. I remember the gleam in her eye. The desire for adventure. How easily she befriended me and was willing to help me. The loyalty and trust.

"I don't know how…"

But she shakes her head. "It is worth the risk for me. I can't stay here." She gestures around as if to encompass the sea. "Tullia has ruined this place. She ruins everything she touches. It's only a matter of time before she ruins me too." She bows her head.

I don't know how it will work. I don't even know if it can be done. But like I said, too much taking and not enough giving. It's a risk. Or a leap of faith, depending on how you look at it. Besides, you can never have too many friends.

"Okay. Okay, Cerise. I'll take you back with me. But I can't make any promises."

She lifts her eyes and the sparkle is almost blinding. She throws her arms around my shoulders. "Thank you." Her voice comes out small sounding. I recognize that tone because I've felt it before myself. She knows she has made the right choice, but a small part of her isn't so sure.

She holds the paper in front of her. "I will need a dagger."

Instead of asking the logical question of *why*, I instead reply. "I lost mine."

She reaches behind her neck and pulls something hidden from inside her hair, then holds it out. It's a silver blade with a gleaming gemstone handle. "You mean this?"

Qildor's dagger. I'm awestruck.

"How'd you do that? Where'd you find it?"

"I tied it up in my hair. That's what I do if I find interesting things that I don't want to lose."

"That's weird, but understandable." Mermaid. No pockets.

"And I found it not that far from where I found you." She glances at the paper. "Okay, we're ready to begin. Hold his hand."

"Is that part of the enchantment?"

She levels me with a very serious stare. "No. That's because I want him to know you're there." She scooches closer, hovering over his body. I take the piece of paper when she hands it to me and slip it back into my bag. Then I take Sloan's hand with my non-charred one and intertwine his fingers in mine as best as I can despite the webbing.

Cerise takes a deep breath and begins to recite the enchantment. The words are beautiful and lyrical. They make no sense to my ears, but it doesn't matter because the effect is an immediate sense of serenity. I'm pretty sure if flowers could talk, then this is what they would sound like. Water begins to swirl around us and I glance at Cerise, but she only nods continuing to recite. She holds her arms over her head as if in a victory. Or a summoning. I grip Sloan's hand tighter. What have I asked her to do?

The water swirls faster and faster around, encircling the three of us. The dagger is in her right hand, high above her head. Then before my brain can make sense of it, she brings the dagger down in a swift arc and plunges the blade into her hip. I let out a cry of protest. But she only shakes her head and continues to recite-sing, the words swirling around us with the current. Purple droplets of blood spill out of her pearlescent-scaled tail and they fall onto Sloan's body. As they do, it's as if they have a mind of their own and begin running across his body, creating rivulets and pathways. His eyelids flutter in response and his lips part. Cerise continues to sing. The water begins to rush around us, thunderous in my ears, drowning out her voice.

I watch as the purple rivulets run down Sloan's torso and down each leg, just as another one runs upward, down his arms and over his neck. The hair on the back of my neck prickles. Something feels different. I can feel it in the water. I hear Altair snort in protest. Sloan's closed eyes flutter faster and faster.

"Now!" Cerise cries, but it's swallowed up by the rushing of water. I look at her over Sloan's awakening body. I shake my head. Purple blood continues to drip out from around the dagger, which she hasn't removed from her hip. Her eyes are unafraid. And perhaps that is what scares me the most. Now, I understand why I was afraid to come here. Water is life. But water is also death. Bubbles of water begin to wrap themselves around Cerise, streams of it tightening around her arms and around her neck. I reach across Sloan, take his other hand and shove it into Cerise's. Once I'm sure she's gripping his fingers, I use the thumb of my injured hand to turn the turquoise and metal ring that rests on my index finger. I close my eyes.

Home, I think. Mom. Dad. Sloan. Safe. A pink, sandy beach. Calm, cerulean water. Blue skies and a single sun. Billions of stars. A hand warm in mine. Up to our knees in the water, dancing. Laughing. Promises yet to be filled and promises already kept. Life and death. But love, always love. Take me home.

Save me.

Save us.

. . .

We land in a tangled crash. I can feel the cool, stone floor beneath my cheek. I am still squeezing Sloan's hand in a death grip.

"Kata! Is that you?" I can hear my mother's bare feet running into the room, probably from the garden. She gasps.

I struggle to my feet, being dropped like that tends to knock the wind out of you. Sloan's eyes are closed but he looks better. There's a flush to his cheeks. His chest rises and falls as if he's sleeping. The scales that were beginning to cover his body are gone. Only. All of his scales are gone and no gills are on either side of his neck. His skin is peachy bronze, smooth and perfect. I trace my finger along his jaw. Did Cerise and I drain him of his Element?

Cerise.

She's splayed across the floor on her back, long red hair somehow wrapped around her body as if she is wearing it. Except. Long, slender, porcelain-skinned legs peek out from between the strands. Her eyes flutter and she groans, clawing at her hip bone. I scramble around Sloan, peeling back the thick, red hair that's covering where she drove the dagger into her hip. It's still there, so deep that all that sticks out is the jewel-encrusted hilt caked in blood.

"Mom," I choke out.

"Oh, dear." My mother kneels on the other side of Cerise. All mom, no goddess. She runs her hands along Cerise's face. Cerise groans again. "You have to pull it out, Kata. I'll go get some bandages." That's the thing about my mom. She doesn't ask questions. Even when I make all the wrong choices, she is always there to try and help me pick up the pieces and put them back together. But I can't help the gnawing feeling. Did she know about Tullia? Did she realize what we were risking going to the Land of Water? But what choice did we have? I brush my fingers over the Water stone resting in my pocket. I still have to destroy it. But first things, first.

"Cerise, I'm going to pull out the dagger." I try to keep my voice calm. Probably not doing a very good job, because Cerise groans even louder.

"You helped me. Now, let me help you." She nods her head ever so slightly and my mom comes running back into the room, hands full of first-aid items. At one time we had the Wood stone and it contained a healing nectar. That also happens to be what made Li immortal, but the stone was destroyed in order to restore that missing piece of me back to its rightful place. This will have to be done the old-fashioned way.

"On the count of three," I instruct. "One." This is impossible. I grip the dagger. "Two." Did Cerise somehow know that the dark enchantment would make her a human being? I recall the assuredness with which she asked for me to take her too. "Three." I pull it out as fast as I can, stumbling back onto my butt in the process. My mother immediately swoops in with a white towel that she presses into Cerise's hip wound, covering the gaping hole left by the dagger. The towel immediately turns red. Except. I look at the dagger in my hand. It too is dripping red. No more purple blood. What have I done?

CHAPTER 16

"They'll be okay."

I am standing in the hallway, looking at Cerise, now outfitted in a pair of my pajamas, red hair splayed down the side of the bed and almost to the floor, in one bedroom and Sloan in the other. He looks so different with his scales gone, as if that was a defining characteristic of who he is. In a way I suppose it was, when it takes up a third of your face.

"You don't know that for sure," I reply. My mother puts a warm hand on my shoulder.

"We have things to discuss."

I sigh and follow her back down the hallway, down the wide steps, through the kitchen and out into the garden. The sun is shining and I can hear birds chirping. The cheeriness wouldn't seem so jarring if not for all that's just happened. "Sit." I sigh again and sit on a bench flanking the long wooden table that runs the length of the pergola. I rest my head in my hands. Sleep pushes in from the edges of my brain. But I know that I can't sleep yet.

"Tell me what happened."

I'm not sure if it's that I don't want to talk about it or if it's too much to tell. I am feeling a plethora of emotions. A bit anger and betrayal mixed with worry and sadness. The anger seems to edge out the other emotions. So I decide to go with angry.

"You knew." I whisper. Somehow it has a more deadening effect on my mother's eyes than if I had yelled it. Her gray eyes turn charcoal.

"I knew Tullia was not a nice person."

I laugh. "Person is generous, don't you think? More like monster."

"I didn't think that she'd try to hurt you."

"Technically, I suppose she didn't hurt *me*. She just tried to seduce my boyfriend with an enchantment, then try to have sex with him so that he'd be cursed and turned into a merman and have to stay there with her forever."

"Sloan will be okay. He's strong."

"Whatever Cerise and I did. His Water. It's gone."

"You saved him."

"What if he's not the same?"

"Li's the same," she points out. And I can't argue there. At first he wasn't. But he's come around. The image of him standing with a bow and arrow, with a beautiful red-haired girl—*Cerise*—by his side drifts back to me. I blink it away.

"Tell me about Cerise." My mother can invade my thoughts like Sloan can, but I know she also realizes that she's treading on dangerous ground here. I don't hide my emotions well. If you want to know how I feel, my face happily broadcasts it for the entire Universe. There's no hiding my true emotions.

"Sloan and I were looking around some shipwrecks for the Water stone. We split up to make it go faster."

"Did you find it?" she interrupts.

I pull it out from my pocket and toss it on the table between us. Smooth, oval, and opalescent in the middle of the whitewashed table.

"Then one of Tullia's pets, a lovely kraken, snatched me up and almost squeezed the life out of me. Cerise found me. She...wasn't like that when she found me."

"Like what?"

I think of the ruby red blood dripping off the tip of the dagger.

"Human."

My mother's eyes widen. "She was a mermaid?"

I shrug. "She never gave me an official title."

"It would seem that the sacrifice of Cerise's mermaid blood, somehow emptied both of them of their Water." She taps her chins as if deep in thought. "That's a bit...unexpected. Where was it that the enchantment came from? The one that saved Sloan."

I wave my hand in the air. "From a dream. Bina gave it to me and said it would save the one I loved. It was in a language that I couldn't read, but Cerise could." My mother's eyes glimpse my hand and I follow her gaze. I forgot about my blackened skin that runs up to my elbow. Shamefully, I shove my arm beneath the table and sit on my hand. Only two fingers can feel the weight of my body pressing into the bench. She narrows her eyes.

"What happened to Tullia?"

I shrug apathetically. "She had a bit of a Fire."

"Kata."

"Mom, don't bother. It doesn't matter. She's immortal and she has her pet, Ridge, to take care of her. I'm sure he's already found her and she's laying in her gigantic bed recuperating until she can trap her next victim." Nightfall pops into my mind then. I wonder if the enchantment did anything to him and the others. I imagine it could have taken him home. But to what? Earth doesn't even exist anymore. Helene is long dead. I swallow. For all I know Nightfall could now be dead too.

Mother presses her lips. I know that means she wants to continue that line of thinking about her sister, but that for now she'll let it rest. I've won, at least temporarily.

"Where's Dad?" I ask.

In the various Lands and in the Elemental Abyss itself, time works differently. It may seem like days have passed, only for you to return to Xon 9 and find out only a few hours have actually passed. That's why being here is so strange. We could be here weeks and go back to the colony and it could be that only a couple of days have passed. It's hard to keep track of something as abstract as time.

Finally, she bites her lip and sighs. Before she says the words I seem to know them already. And I'm no mind-reader. "He hasn't come back yet." My stomach clenches and my heart sinks. Sloan and I were gone two days. If Water time and Earth time operate the same way, then Dad should have returned by now.

"We have to go find him."

"I know," she sighs. "Rest, Kata. You need it as much as Sloan and Cerise. We'll see how they fair tomorrow. And then…" Her voice trails off and I know it's because she can't come with us. The agreement between Raj and Katayun with my mother—when she wanted to become mortal and live on Xon 9 just for a little while (because that's what a human life span is when you're eternal, a blip on the Universal radar)—was that when she left she could never go back.

I nod sleepily and push myself up from the table. It doesn't make any sense. I saw Li and Ahna in my dreams. They were both fine. But then where was my father? And why hadn't he returned yet? Except. I recall Ahna's yellow eye looking back at me. The Imminent Darkness. As I grow stronger it grows weaker. But then it's forced to feed. I rub the Water stone between my fingers as I make my way up the steps. I need to destroy it. I also need to find my father. And I can't do it alone.

My body automatically walks me past my room. I look in at Cerise, like a sleeping angel, her serene face and strawberry-colored hair draped all around her. The pearlescent quality of her skin is gone, and yet she still seems radiant. Some girls must just be lucky, I guess.

I turn into Sloan's room. He's lying on his back, brown hair making a jagged line across his forehead. I make my way to the bed and lay down carefully beside him, placing one of his arms beneath my neck and curling up into him, my knees pressed against his hip bone. I place my hand that still holds the Water stone over his chest, waiting until I feel the soft rhythm of his heartbeat. I kiss his cheek, where the familiar silver-green scales used to be. Soft, supple skin melts into my lips.

. . .

The first thing I notice upon waking is that I didn't dream. The second thing I notice is the space beside me is empty. The sheets are cool to my touch. Warm, golden light streams in from the row of windows to my right. I scratch the sleep from my eyes and push myself into a sitting position. I kind of wish it all had been a dream. I'm not necessarily looking forward to what today will bring. Or tomorrow. Or even the day after that. With the Imminent Darkness pulling the strings, the days are full of the dangerously unexpected. I used to hate that I was ordinary. Now, I wish that I was.

Once my eyes adjust to the room's brightness, I see that Sloan is at the foot of the bed, staring into a mirror that hangs above a dresser. He's inspecting the right side of his face, running a hand over his smooth, scale-free skin. His fingers move to his neck where he pokes at where his gills used to wiggle, signaling his need to restore his Water equilibrium. He notices my reflection in the mirror and turns leaning against the dresser. I brace myself for a barrage of accusations, but I should know better. Accusations aren't Sloan's way.

He shrugs and gives me an unsure smile. "Well, this is unexpected."

I finger the pale yellow sheets cautiously. "How much do you remember?"

He scratches his chin thoughtfully. "I remember the ship graveyard and splitting up to look for the Water stone. Then I thought I heard you call my name. It sounded like you were in trouble, so I found and mounted Altair, then we followed the sound. It was only a little bit away, near an outcropping of fallen over stones. When we got there, you looked as if you'd been injured. It was hard to tell."

"But it wasn't me," I clarify. My stomach clenches. Some stupid enchantment wasn't enough? Tullia had to trick Sloan by pretending to *be* me too?

His eyes simmer with regret. "I know that now." He crosses the space between us in a single step, and sits at the edge of the bed. "Ka, I am so sorry for what I did. Whatever you think I did."

"You didn't know what you were doing! It was Tullia's stupid enchantment!" I protest. My words are fierce because it's the truth.

"I should have been stronger. It doesn't excuse what happened."

This is all wrong. He should be furious at me. Furious for me taking away his Water, for leaving him hollowed out and emptied. This should not be him apologizing to me.

"What exactly happened?" My voice comes out small sounding.

He puts a hand on my leg and I can feel its warmth permeating the sheet. He closes his eyes as if trying to remember. "When I bent over to see if you—well, Tullia pretending to be you—were alright, her eyes were completely black and for a second I knew. Just knew. But it's like even if my head and heart wanted to stop it, my body couldn't. She took me back to the castle." He swallows and it's audible in the silence. I watch the rise and fall of his Adam's apple. "The rest is kind of fuzzy."

"Did you...?" It's a stupid question. It doesn't matter, does it? Just because it hadn't happened between us yet. But the thought of Tullia and Sloan together in that way makes me sick to my stomach. Even if it was all a trick or an illusion to Sloan, the reality of it is still the same.

He sighs, shoulders slumped. "I don't remember."

Sloan doesn't lie. I think of my heart pounding in my chest when I found Tullia on top of him, both shirtless, her bare chest pressed against his. The flick of her forked black tongue. Will I ever be able to get that image out of my head? Honestly, I'm not sure.

"Well," I reason, avoiding his eyes. Running my finger back and forth across the satin seam of the sheet. "Perhaps if you had...we wouldn't have been able to save you. You'd have that tattoo curse dancing across your skin and you'd be a merman trapped with Tullia forever. But you're not. You're here. With me." I can't hide the hope from my voice.

His hand stops mine, enclosing around it. "Who's we?"

Of all the things to say or ask, I hate that he attacks the most logical and obvious thing. But that's typical Sloan. He always needs concrete proof and evidence before he draws a conclusion. I gesture at the closed bedroom door. "Across the hall. Her name is Cerise. It's kind of a complicated story. But we used a dark enchantment—one that Bina told me about in a dream." I leave out the part about it being in a book of my entire life. The Book of Ka. The Book of the Impossible Girl. Sloan's brow furrows as he tries to understand. I continue, "At the graveyard, a kraken found me. I thought they were only made up."

Sloan's laugh is scornful. "You should know by now that fantasy and reality bleed together. At least around here."

I nod. "I got away, but I was hurt. And a mermaid saved me. Her name is Cerise." Sloan narrows his eyes suspiciously, and after his experience with Tullia, I'd say rightfully so. "No, she's nice. I swear. And…I'd seen her before." I shake my head. "That part doesn't matter. She's not a mermaid anymore anyways."

Sloan cocks an eyebrow. The sunlight reflects in his eyes, making them sparkle like the most pristine emeralds. With or without scales, he's beautiful. "And what is she now?"

"A human, I guess." Now he raises both eyebrows in disbelief. "I'm not exactly sure how it happened, she may be better able to explain it. She was injured, but I think she's better now. We could go wake her."

"I think it could wait a few more moments," he replies.

I don't mention that my father hasn't returned. Time is different here. We have this moment. We have time to try and make things right. Sloan leans back on one elbow, a lock of hair falls across his forehead. My heart pounds in my chest. He runs a hand tentatively over my leg that's beneath the sheet, stopping at the top of my thigh. My breath catches in my throat. I raise my eyes to his and am relieved to only see green and a small, black pupil looking back. This isn't the enchantment.

"I really am sorry, Ka." He pulls his hand away as if suddenly ashamed. "I only hope that you can forgive me. I'd never hurt you on purpose."

Without thinking I throw my arms around his neck and he pulls me down to him. His hands run through my hair and over the tattoo on the back of my neck, lips skimming my chin until they find my lips. I press back into him. I want him to be angry at me. Somehow, I feel like it would take away some of the guilt that I feel. I want to tell him that I forgive him, but what is there to forgive? Is forgiveness needed when someone uses someone else's body to commit a transgression? He kisses my shoulder. I close my eyes, expecting to see the image that I can't seem to shake, but instead I just see Sloan, feel his arms around me, and smell the salty and fresh air that clings to his hair and skin. Once he understands that his Water has been completely drained, it will be my turn to ask for forgiveness. Because that's what true love is, isn't it? Loving the person enough to seek their forgiveness. And being loving enough to give it.

CHAPTER 17

There's a crash from upstairs. Sloan, Mom, and I are clustered around the kitchen table with the Water stone in between us. We simultaneously look up at the sound. Sloan raises an eyebrow. Strands of red hair appear followed by porcelain fingers gripping the elaborate iron handrail. Long, pale legs follow. Cerise clings to the handrail as if her life depends on it. She wobbles down the steps like a toddler. She's wearing a pair of my shorts and a t-shirt, looking decidedly un-mermaid-like.

I get up when she reaches the bottom and sling an arm around her waist to help guide her to the table.

"I don't know how you guys make this look so easy!"

"I've had about eighteen years of practice," I reply. She sits in my seat and her hazel eyes immediately narrow in on the Water stone in all its opalescent rainbow glory. Tentatively, she runs a finger over it.

In addition to legs, Cerise has experienced a couple of other transformations. Where there was once no nose, is now a pert little slope. Two faded lines on either cheek are the only indication of the gills that were once there.

Sloan clears his throat.

"Oh. Yeah. Cerise, you've already met Sloan. Sort of. And this is my mom, Novea." My mother has many names: Novea, Kesara, Anuja. But I just stick with what I've always known. It's less confusing that way. Even if she does look slightly different in her reincarnated form, she's still my mom. Sometimes frustratingly so.

"It's nice to meet you, Cerise." Mom's brow furrows. I know that she wants to question Cerise and find out how it is exactly she came to be human and how Sloan was drained of his Water. How she knew that it was a dark enchantment, and more importantly how she knew that it would even work. But there are other more pressing things that need our attention at the moment.

"Is that the Water stone?" Cerise asks. "The one that you were looking for when Tullia's kraken found you?"

I pick it up turning it between my index and middle fingers. Today, I put on a long-sleeved shirt that covers part of my hand and has thumbholes. I'd rather not think about the dead skin running up my arm. I assume it will heal eventually, being half-immortal. Then again, it was caused by immortal magic. So maybe I'll be like this forever. I push the thought aside. More important things.

"Now, I have to destroy it."

Cerise scrunches up her face. "Why would you want to destroy something so beautiful?" I give Cerise the short version of why I was in the Land of Water in the first place. She doesn't ask many questions. I suppose when you live in a place where magic is around you all the time, there isn't much that surprises you anymore.

"It's how I restore that part of my personality," I conclude.

"In order to protect Kata, a part of her personality was trapped inside each of the stones. This was how we tricked the Imminent Darkness for so long." My mom explains, the *we* referring to her and Sloan's own mother, Bina. "I should have known it wouldn't last forever."

"They grow up so fast don't they?" I ask sarcastically. This has been harder on me more than anyone.

"How will you destroy it?" Cerise asks, not noticing the sarcasm. Of course, I wouldn't exactly expect a mermaid to be fluent in sarcasm.

I walk over to my messenger bag, which sits on the kitchen counter. It's really seen better days. There's a patched hole from when the Fire stone burned through it, numerous loose threads, and a frayed seam. Not to mention it now smells like something went rancid. A weird combination of smoke, dead leaves, and salt water. I lift the flap and pull out the sack Bina gave me on my second visit. I bring it to the table and unceremoniously dump its contents next to the Water stone.

"These are the only objects I have left. There was a vial of an acidic substance and a speckled feather, but I used those already. Sometimes the objects literally destroy the stone, and sometimes they're just a tool to help it along."

Sloan picks up the matches from The Old Tavern and the Sea, turning them in his hand, inspecting the front and back of the packet. He's seen the pack before, once when we were trying to destroy the Fire stone and again in the amber mines in the Land of Wood. But now his forehead is wrinkled as if deep in thought. After our conversation, this morning he's been quiet. Perhaps the reality of the situation and the cost of the trip to the Land of Water finally sinking in. I didn't think things would go back to normal that easily. If there's one thing I've learned, it's that change is the only thing that can be counted on.

"This place sounds familiar," he says finally. Cerise has picked up the brilliantly, clear crystal and is studying it with a mesmerized expression.

"Is it in the Black Bazaar?"

"No. No, I don't think so. It's on Xon 9 though."

My mother interjects. "I've heard of it too. I think it's on the other side of the University Complex." Mom was a researcher in the Earth Building. She studied food shortages and population control. Trying to learn from Old Earth's mistakes.

Sloan's forehead unfurrows. "Yes. I think that's where I've heard of it before. From other students when I was at University." He looks up at me. "We should check it out."

I nod. "But first…"

"Your father."

"And Li. And Ahna. And Doran. And Bina." I correct. This

morning I'd told Sloan about my dream. At least the part about Ahna.

I amend, "Everyone. It's been too long. If the Imminent Darkness has infiltrated the Black Bazaar, how long until it has permeated the entire colony?" My question hides my true concern. What about my friends? I want—no, *need*—my friends to help me. I need them by my side. I can't do all this alone. I don't *want* to do all this alone. Worse, what if something has happened to them? It would somehow be my fault. The Imminent Darkness being here now, is my fault. I could never just accept that I was ordinary. But how do you accept a lie?

"What's the Imminent Darkness?" Cerise asks, not looking up from the crystal.

"It's energy," my mother explains. "A very archaic form of energy. When Raj and Katayun created the Universe, there needed to be rules. The natural law of creation demanded it. Bring in the Imminent Darkness. It can take many forms: human, animal, the smallest microbe. But it's too flamboyant to be something so small. It likes to be seen."

"And when I was born, to an immortal mother and a mortal father, it threw the Universe off balance. The Imminent Darkness is looking to restore that balance. Unfortunately, it has some not so nice ways of trying to do it."

"As Ka restores her personality, which is the core of each Element, she grows stronger and the Imminent Darkness grows weaker. In order to gain strength, it feeds off energy. Like a parasite, when it takes that energy, every negative quality about a person seems to dominate. Paranoia, aggression, distrust, cruelty…it's not pretty," Sloan adds.

Cerise shudders. "How do you stop such a thing?"

Sloan and I exchange a glance. "We aren't completely sure yet."

The four of us sit in silence for a few moments. I scoop the matches and the crystal back into the little, burlap sack then tuck the Water stone securely in my pants pocket. I can feel the coolness permeate the fabric as it presses against my hip bone. Each stone has not only looked different, but *felt* different. I suppose that's to be expected since each one represents a different Element. The Water stone is beautiful on the outside, but I'm not so sure if it's as beautiful on the inside. Kind of like its queen. At the thought, a tiny bubble of anger rises inside me. I pop it before I say something I might regret.

"So, how do we find your father?" Cerise asks.

"We're going back to the colony. It's the last place we know that he went."

Cerise voices the concern that the rest of us don't want to say out loud. Saying things out loud makes them seem so much more real. "And if he's not there?"

"We keep looking." Sloan catches my eye across the table and I nod.

"We keep looking."

· · ·

The way to get to the various lands from Xon 9 was through the

Elemental Abyss. There were five doors, each one a portal leading to the lands of Earth, Water, Fire, Wood, and Metal. Except now the Elemental Abyss has been destroyed, its positive magic poisoned by the Imminent Darkness. That doesn't leave many options. I have my ring of course, but that's like a one-way ticket. It only brings me home. My dad had his watch, its living memory recalling the last place that it was. And my mother has a key. She presses it into my hand now.

"The Elemental Abyss would be too dangerous."

"If it still exists," I correct as I double check the contents of my bag: water, nutrient pills, flashlight, sack from Bina, and a jacket. The temperature of Xon 9 is a constant, comfortable 67 degrees. But you never know where you could end up, especially when you find out there are portals to other lands and that time could pass differently depending on where you are.

I join Sloan and Cerise in the kitchen. It's taken me all morning to try and get used to Sloan's changed face, but it still takes my breath away whenever I look at him. This must be what he looked like before his Pronouncement. After Pronouncement they induce the Change with an injection. It's easier, more efficient. And helps control the chosen Element. It's only one of the ways we've tried to harness the powers of our strange planet. Somehow the scaly mark of Water had made him seem wiser, older. Now, he looks young and fresh-faced. He catches me looking and runs a hand self-consciously along the side of his face.

We stand in a small circle: Sloan, Cerise, and myself. My mother on the outside. Cerise has changed into a pair of my boots, jeans and a sweatshirt. She somehow manages to make it look elegant instead of frumpy. Her wavy red hair has been twisted into a long braid. I grab one of Cerise's hands and Sloan mimics the gesture. I take my hand with the key pressed into its palm and grab Sloan's free hand. Immediately, it's like the world is sliding in on itself, folding over on us.

We're hurtling through time and space. Blackness surrounds us. I can't physically feel either Sloan or Cerise. But I know that they're there because of the images. They flash in front of my eyes like an old movie reel. Cerise's confusion as she stumbles upon my body. Sloan's look of panic as he searches for me among the wrecked ships of the graveyard. Nightfall's tears falling onto the glass of a gilded picture frame, before floating up and away sucked up into the ocean. Tullia looking down at me—Sloan, blonde hair like a curtain as she runs her hands over the sides of my face. There's no sound, but I can read her lips: *Pretty, pretty.*

This is the part of teleportation I could do without. My stomach rounds on itself, except I don't know if it's the momentary sensation of nothingness: just memories and thoughts—none of which are mine—floating through the ether, or if it's the image of Tullia with Sloan. I know that Sloan and Cerise are being bombarded with images as well, and that's no comfort either.

A pinprick of light begins to grow and the images stop, as if the reel has been broken. The light grows brighter until it's almost blinding and then it seems to swallow us whole before spitting us out on the other side. We fall out in a tumble of arms and legs. The key falls out of my palm with a thump to the floor. It takes a minute to recover, having the wind knocked out of you. I've landed on worse though.

I push myself up to a seated position, allowing my eyes to adjust to the dim light. The earthy smell of moss and dirt, edged with the metallic scent of blood hits me. I look down and I'm sitting in a deep, dark stain on the tan-colored carpet. I back pedal, sliding across the floor on my butt, hands and heels until my back hits the wall. My breath comes in short, panicked gasps. It's not fresh. It's an old stain, I remind myself.

We landed in my mother's office. Of course we did, because that's what the key remembers last. It remembers my mother bleeding on the floor, a hooded figure leaving her to die. Even though my brain knows that my mother is safe and that she's in another place, it doesn't slow the rapid thump of my heart. I feel frozen to the spot, my knees curled into my chest. The key rests in the center of that dark stain, the reminder of the danger to those that I love. The house heaves around me, as if it too feels my pain. The silence would be deafening if not for the rush of blood in my ears.

Suddenly, Sloan is crouched in front of me. His face is pale and angular, his brow furrowed in concern. He doesn't touch me. In a voice calm as the sea at sunset, he says softly. "It's over. That was the past, Kata. It is not now."

Not now. Not now. I rock back and forth, letting my head hit the wall behind me with a soft thud. Over and over again. *Not now. Not now.* That was the past. *Past. Past. Past.* My eyes burn and my nose begins to tingle. The tears push out and roll down my cheek before I can stop them. Hanging for a moment at my chin, as if suspended in time, before dropping to my t-shirt.

Sloan reaches out and brushes them away with his thumbs. He lets me fold myself into his arms and I press my eyes into his shoulders. He rocks me carefully back and forth. *The past, the past, the past.* I hear Cerise pick up the key and then she is beside me too. She wraps an arm around my shoulders, pressing her back against the wall. She doesn't know what happened here, but I suppose it doesn't take a genius to figure out it was something bad. Her voice is barely above a whisper, when she asks, "Where are we?"

"This is Kata's house. Her mom's office." Sloan's voice is soft and gentle. I inhale the mix of sea salt and soap from his hair and skin. My heart begins to slow down. The rush of blood becomes a trickle. Cerise must glance at the old blood stain because Sloan continues, "Her mother was attacked by the Imminent Darkness here. Not the creature itself, but the humans who help it do its work. The humans that it feeds off of. The key remembered. This is the last place it had been."

I take a deep, shuddering breath. It sounds so cool and rational when the words come out of Sloan's mouth. *Not now. Not now.* Finally, I look up, back into the room. My mom's papers are still in disarray, splayed across the floor. The intruder had been looking for something. I don't think he ever found it. The map and key were kept in a secret compartment in one of the desk drawers. There's an overturned chair in the corner. Otherwise, everything is the same. The silence. The emptiness. No voices drifting up from the kitchen below. No more sleepless nights, staring out my bedroom window wondering what the future holds for me. If anything at all. This is no longer home.

As if reading my mind, Cerise gives my shoulder a squeeze. "It's not always about the place. It's about the people."

Sloan pulls me to my feet. I'm compelled to pick up the papers. I begin collecting them into a stack. Wordlessly, Sloan and Cerise begin to help me. Cerise rights the fallen chair and then one by one closes the desk's open drawers. One of the drawers won't close because it's been busted from the intruder's reckless search. Sloan sets the papers in a haphazard pile on the desk. I disappear into the hall closet and bring back a small, woven rug. I drop it to the floor, over the dark stain. If you didn't know, hadn't seen it for yourself, you'd never have known it happened.

"We'll be downstairs?" It's a question, not a statement. I look at Sloan and nod. He gives my hand a squeeze before disappearing with Cerise down the hallway.

I stand in the doorway, taking in the room. A couple potted plants—succulents my mom had called them—line the top of the desk, untouched by the events that took place in the room around it. There's a window above the desk. Pink light filters in through the yellowed curtains, spilling across the desk. Something glitters in the light. At first I think it's a mirror, reflecting the sun's light, but then I notice there's no square of light dancing on the floor or wall next to me. I cross the room to the desk. I don't want to keep Sloan and Cerise waiting. Things to do. Like finding my father. The metallic glint is coming from one of the drawers, which had been placed in askew. It's the broken drawer. I carefully remove it and reach inside, pulling out the metallic object. It's a message tube. I don't know how it could have gotten here.

Its light flashes green.

There's a message.

I tuck it carefully in my pocket next to the Water stone, place the drawer crookedly back in, then leave the room to join Sloan and Cerise downstairs.

CHAPTER 18

Finding my father should take precedence over everything else. But it would be so much easier with more help. I easily convince Sloan that we should go next door and see if Li and Ahna are home. Despite the fact that Ahna's mad at me, I'd be lying if I said we didn't need her help. We stand on the small front stoop. I knock on the front door twice. Cerise is crouched down, digging her fingers into the red soil. She scoops it up into her hands, then lets it sift back down through her fingers.

"This is not sand," she observes.

"No. It's dirt. We don't have surface water here," I explain.

"But if you ever want to go for a swim, I know just the place." Sloan's referring to the pool beneath the Water building, where Water Elementals used to stay in the University Complex. I'm about to point out how all the buildings have been closed, when the front door is yanked open.

Li stands in its opening, black hair askew in every direction. Shirtless, of course, because apparently that's how he rolls these days. His jeans are slung low around his hips. He scratches his chest. A lazy smile spreads across his face.

"Kata." Then his eyes drift over to Sloan. "Sloan. Bro, what happened to your face?"

"We're not here to talk about that. Can we come in?" I ask.

Cerise stands up and Li notices her for the first time. I see the glint in his brown eyes as he takes in her long red hair which she braided over her shoulder, along with her baggy sweatshirt and very long legs. But truly, it's her face that's so arresting. The pouty pink lips and golden, hazel eyes matched with her porcelain skin makes her stunning, despite the fine scars that line either cheek.

"And hello, Beautiful Majesty," Li grins. For the first time I see a light pink creep up Cerise's neck and bloom at her cheeks. "You brought a pet back from the Land of Water."

"She is not a pet, you idiot." I push Li aside, back flush against the door and elbow my way into the house. Sloan follows, then Cerise. Li shuts the door behind us. "And put some clothes on."

The house is dim. All the blinds are drawn shut against the outside world. And frankly, with the Imminent Darkness running around, it isn't a world you want to really let in. Li gestures to the living room and we sit down. He disappears momentarily, then returns pulling a long-sleeved shirt over his head.

"Where's Ahna?" I ask glancing up the steps. All the concrete houses in our neighborhood are laid out the same way. Kitchen and living room downstairs, three bedrooms upstairs.

Li shrugs. "Out. Or something." He hasn't taken his eyes off Cerise. He sits in an armchair across from us, his heels propped up on a wooden table, legs crossed at the ankle. The epitome of relaxed. Not like the entire world as we know it is in danger of being annihilated or anything like that.

"Or something? Liwald Sollomon, you better start giving me some real answers and stop messing around."

He runs a hand through his hair. "Okay, okay. I'm not messing around. I don't know where she's been running off to. She's been different since we came home."

"Different how?" I know he isn't being forthright with me. Ahna's told me before that twins have a special relationship. "Can't you, like, use your twin superpowers to figure it out?"

Li scoffs. "Kata, surely, you know you're the only one amongst us with any super powers." He nods his head toward Cerise. "Aren't you going to introduce us?"

"Maybe if you behave yourself."

He smirks. "I know Ahna was angry about everything that happened. Unlike me, she's not so good at the whole forgive and forget thing. And did I mention, I feel great?" Obviously, since he was wandering around half-naked. His brow furrows and the cocky façade vanishes. "So, are you going to tell me what happened?"

"I got the Water stone. Cerise saved my life. My aunt tried to curse my boyfriend and then Cerise saved his life. Oh, and my father is missing. I think that about covers everything." I glance at Sloan who shrugs a shoulder and gives an indifferent nod.

"First things first. Cerise, it's a pleasure to meet you. And believe me the pleasure is definitely mine. My name's Li. I happen to be Ka's very good-looking best friend. So, it's a good thing you're in the business of saving lives because Ka, here, has almost gotten me killed twice." Cerise's eyebrows shoot up near her hairline. Li puts up a reassuring hand. "Kidding. Sort of." He turns back to me. "Now, what's this about a curse? Is that what happened to your face?" He gestures to Sloan.

"It's the queen," Cerise pipes up. Since she's no longer waterbound, her voice no longer has the same melodious quality. It's still bubbly, but there's a softness around the edges. She glances at me to make sure she's not overstepping any boundaries. New world, possibly new rules. I shake my head, encouraging her to go on. "The Water Queen is evil. Her lust is insatiable. She uses an enchantment that is carried by the water's currents. It makes human men ravenous with longing, but only for her. Once she consummates her desire, the man is then cursed. He begins to turn into a merman and then he is bound to the Land of Water. Forever."

"So, wait. Let me get this straight." Li points to me. "Your aunt tried to seduce your boyfriend and curse him. But obviously, it didn't work because Sloan's here now. Albeit, he doesn't look as handsome as before."

Sloan rolls his eyes. "It didn't work because Ka rescued me." He scratches at his chin which now has a shadow of stubble. "And then

Cerise performed some kind of dark enchantment."

"Yes, a dark enchantment that would turn me human as well. The blood of a mermaid in sacrifice for the life of a man. But it worked out because I'm happy to be rid of that awful place," Cerise says, her smile shy.

"Okay, still trying to follow here. So Ka rescued Sloan and then Cerise saved Sloan's life. Cerise performs some kind of ritual which turned them both completely human. And then Cerise came along for the ride. Have I got that?"

"Pretty much," I say. Admittedly, the story sounds almost ridiculous. Almost.

"That kind of explains what happened to Teach's face. So, he's like me now. His Element is gone." If only Li knew how different they were. An immortal and a mortal. I should tell him. I just don't want him to do anything stupid. Which is a very real possibility when we're talking about Li.

"As far as I know." Sloan rubs the right side of his face. "No scales. No gills."

"Do you feel hollowed out? Empty inside?" Li asks, his own fingers tracing the black filigree along the right side of his face. It's a loaded question. My heart begins to pound in my chest. I assumed that's how Sloan felt because I know that's how Li felt after the incident with the army of Fire. He had literally burned up from the inside out. And it was all my fault. Sloan losing his Water is all my fault too.

"Actually, I feel like I did before the Change. Just…normal." The words are a relief. I'm glad to know that Sloan doesn't feel less than because of what happened. Our Elements are just an affiliation. I'm learning that they're no longer a definition of who we are or who we can be.

Li keeps his eyes on Sloan, as if they're having some kind of telepathic exchange. Who knows? Maybe they are. Finally, Li says, "Me too."

"Okay, now that that's out of the way." I stand up and use my foot to push Li's feet off the table. I sit on it so that I'm facing everyone at once. "Can we talk about my dad?"

"You said he's missing?" Li asks, leaning forward with his elbows on this knees.

"Mom said he never came back after bringing you guys home. The Imminent Darkness already took him once," I say finally giving voice to my unspoken fear. Xon 9 is full of the Imminent Darkness's minions, many of whom aren't even aware that there's an actual force behind their actions. At one point, Sloan had infiltrated their lower ranks in order to learn of their plans, but the only thing he really was able to find out is how secretive it all was. No one seems to know who's in charge, but orders come down nonetheless and are followed. Information is known to only a select few and not readily available to those in the lower ranks.

"Maybe he stopped by the office?" My father was a liege to the Council of Wood. He worked in Council Hall, which, ironically, is where he was kept when he was kidnapped. Beneath the Council Hall was a dark, dank prison where the Imminent Darkness could detain its challengers. The scary part about the Imminent Darkness is that it infiltrates your mind. It takes away all the good and consumes you with all the bad. Before you know what's hit you, you no longer know the difference.

I shake my head. "For what? His life is not here anymore."

"Well, what if he lost his watch? He couldn't get back home then." Li has a point. But if it was just a quick drop-off, then how would he have had time to lose his watch? Except…maybe it wasn't a quick in and out. Maybe Li's right. Maybe he did go somewhere else. But where?

"Okay, then. So we're no longer just looking for your dad, we're looking for a watch with a living memory." Sloan clasps his hands over his knees. "That should be easy." He doesn't try to hide the note of sarcasm. I can't blame him.

"Well, we'd better get moving then. Before we run out of time." Li pauses dramatically awaiting expected accolades for his witty quip.

"Time waits for no man," Sloan adds with a grin.

"Therefore, time must be a woman." I smile. It's good to have friends. Even if their jokes really are super lame.

. . .

The list of places my father could have visited are never ending. He could have gone to Council Hall, although I think it's unlikely. Or he could have gone to the Black Bazaar. Also, unlikely as my parents more or less forbade me to go there. Not that I listened. Or he could have gone to the University Complex. Except for the small fact that it was shut down until further notice. That doesn't leave many other options.

"He could have gone to Mrs. Chatfield's," Sloan suggests, referring to Doran's mother's safe house on the edges of the Underground.

"Yeah, if the Imminent Darkness hadn't already driven them out of it. The Underground is all but abandoned," Li reminds us.

"True. I'm running out of ideas," I groan. Trying not to let the panic coat my voice. Sloan gives my elbow a reassuring squeeze, and I know that he's dipped into my own thoughts and seen the long, crossed-off list of places Dad could have gone.

"What about the military complex? Or to Bina's?" Li asks.

"It's possible. I guess we have to visit Bina anyways. Make sure she's okay. Maybe she knows something about Dad." Unless Dad visited her, the only way she'd know is if she used her Sight. One of the few gifts that was not passed onto Sloan. What will she say when she sees his scale-less face? Sloan's grip around me tightens.

"We can check on Michaela too."

There's a slight edge to his voice when he says his sister's name. Let's just say that we used to sort of be friends, but once she found out who I was and what Sloan was to me that ended pretty quickly. I can't blame her for not being a fan of a girl who's constantly putting both her brother and mother in danger. A lot like Ahna, the only difference being that in the past, Michaela has threatened to turn me in to the military. I'm not exactly sure what she thinks that would do. It wouldn't stop the Imminent Darkness. The ID would just cause them to turn against one another and use their own weapons on each other. It's not something that can be shot or even killed for that matter. It's something that needs to be bottled up and put away. Controlled. Forever.

There aren't many people out as we head across the colony. Everyone has scurried away and hid from the colonists who've aligned with the Imminent Darkness, a force so great they could never even truly understand the sort of evil with which they've decided to pledge their allegiance. The Imminent Darkness is every bad thing you can think of. It's every nightmare, every sin, and every lie. It's hurtful words, dishonest actions, and destructive thoughts. It's not something anyone of sound mind would want to be a part of. Then again, when the ID's involved, the whole idea of a sound mind goes out the window. It whispers silently in your ear until your mind is all jumbled up and your sense of right and wrong becomes twisted. Manipulation. Deception. Corruption.

As we walk, I notice that something looks different. Besides the lack of people. At first I can't place my finger on it. Then I realize that it's the plants. The once silvery foliage that skimmed the ground now have blackened tips, curling back on itself. Silver leaves that once reached for the red sun are now dead and black, crunching beneath our boots.

"What's wrong with this place?" Cerise asks. Her voice is barely above a whisper.

"The Imminent Darkness." I stop walking, squat, and rub a spindly plant between my index finger and thumb. It crumbles easily, leaving a jagged line. "This is what it does. To the plants, to the mind.

To the world." I stand back up. I'm a bit sorry I've pulled Cerise into this mess. She's traded one horrible place for another.

Li's brow is furrowed, but he doesn't say anything. Before the incident, he used to always have a quip—a smart remark for everything. But now his quips are fewer, and his silences are more. He often seems lost in his own deep thoughts, occasionally snapping out of it with a smile. We continue walking past the Black Bazaar. No sounds greets us. No smells drift down the alleyway toward us. The old wooden sign that used to be staked into the ground is long gone. Normally, we would cut through the Black Bazaar to get to the other side of the Underground. Not today.

Suddenly, Li says, "Let's go this way." He's pointing to the alleyway.

"We can't go that way. Doran told us, and we saw for ourselves the last time, that the Imminent Darkness has been there. It's not safe," I object. Cerise peers down the alleyway, which is made of cobblestones and leads to steps that open up on a world of metal trailers that turn into vendors when the moons rise. Forbidden food and drink, fortunes told, tattoos, and stolen kisses. I experienced a lot of firsts at the Black Bazaar. Almost all of them with Li. But that was then and this is now.

"It's quicker," he replies simply. I look up at the sky. Since time is different here than the Land of Earth, I wasn't sure what time it was when we arrived. But now the twin moons are just beginning to rise over the horizon. And there's a curfew now, a poor effort from the Council of Leaders to try and stop the burglaries and kidnappings conducted by the Imminent Darkness.

I sigh. "Okay. Fine." Sloan gives me a look and I shrug helplessly, because for once Li is right. It makes the most sense.

Li leads the way down the narrow cobblestone street. As soon as we reach the end of the alleyway a stifling smell hits my nostril. It's a mix of something both rotting and burning. I slip my hand into Sloan's. We pass Bina's trailer, now dark and abandoned, which was near the entrance. All the trailers have their metal gates pulled down. A sole neon sign, half-burned out, flashes. Smart as he is, Li sticks to the shadows cast by the trailers to our right. It isn't complete coverage, but it helps and makes it easier to slip in between two vendors if we need to hide from view.

The street is lined with trash: papers, half-eaten food, bottles, and smashed trinkets. One of the lamp posts is burned out and the bench beneath it has a curled up form on it. Someone probably sleeping and waiting for the nighttime debauchery to begin. It doesn't take long before we find the source of the smell. A few yards down from the sleeper is a metal trash bin. Its contents have been lit on fire and the flames are going strong. The temperature never changes, so it surely isn't needed for warmth. Maybe to cook something. But not likely.

"What's going on?" I press against Sloan's shoulder and whisper into his ear. We've stopped walking, and stand in the shadows watching the flames lick, leap, and dance.

"I'm not sure," he replies. His voice is calm. Typical Sloan. We tend to be the opposite of one another at any given time. "It could be a ritual or it could be…a practicality."

"Do you really think that it's trash that they're burning?"

Li overhears me. "Not trash." He closes his eyes and inhales. As far as I know, immortality did not come with other heightened senses. Just a very, very, very long existence. He opens one eye. "Can't you smell it?"

I close my eyes and flare my nostrils, trying to suck in as much of the putrid air as possible in order to decipher the smell. If I concentrate, I can discern the scent of burning papers mixed in with the smell of burned food. But there's something else. Something metallic that stands out. I can't place what it is.

"Blood." Li says by way of explanation.

"Blood?" Cerise repeats. Half her face is hidden by the shadows and her eyes dance with the reflection of the flames.

"What does that mean?" I ask.

"It means sacrifice," Sloan says slowly.

"Exactly," Li grimaces rubbing his chin. "Only is it a willing sacrifice?" He glances at Cerise who still stares off into the immediate distance as if entranced. "Or an unwillingly sacrifice?"

As if in answer to his question, there's a shuffling noise followed by a dragging sound. Several hooded figures have emerged. I don't notice from where. In between them is a shadowy figure, hands and feet bound with rope. The binds cause the person to continually stumble and fall, only to be kicked by one of the hooded figures and then dragged back up to his feet. The person is tall and slender. I catch a glimpse of a defiant jaw, jutted upward. My heart sinks. I'd recognize that jawline anywhere.

Li pulls us further into the blanket of shadows. We stand and watch as the cloaked figures form a semi-circle around the burning trash bin. One of the figures pushes forth the prisoner and my heart bursts against my ribcage in recognition.

"Is that...?" Sloan asks.

I close my eyes against the burn of tears and nod. "Doran."

CHAPTER 19

I hold my breath as I watch one of the cloaked figures pull out a sleek, shiny dagger. This is unlike Sloan's dagger which is nestled inside my stinky messenger bag. It isn't bejeweled with gemstones, and I highly doubt it was gifted to the owner by an actual Wood elf. Instead, this weapon is constructed for inflicting maximum pain. The steel blade glints in the dim light of the fire.

"I'm not going to ask you again," says one of the figures in a low voice. Their faces are hidden in the shadows of their hoods, but the voice sounds familiar.

I glance at Sloan and he nods. He recognizes it too.

Doran lunges forward, but he's bound and held by another figure, so he only moves about an inch. Realizing his movement's ineffectiveness, he spits at the feet of the person who spoke.

"Very well, then. Loosen the rope." The figure holding the ropes obliges, loosening the ropes in such a way that the figure who speaks is able to grab Doran's hand and yank him forward, toward the fire. The fire glints off something metallic, shiny and silver. On Doran's wrist I can see an illuminated sapphire blue face. My father's watch. But how did Doran get it? "Perhaps this will entice you to speak." He takes the tip of the dagger and drags it along the inside of Doran's forearm. He gasps in pain.

When I first met Doran after the Ritual of Fire, if I'm being honest, I thought he was a complete jerk. But then I discovered his true nature after he'd been tortured by Tristen. He'd been vulnerable, and yet still refused to let me in. It took a lot of time, and a trip through the Elemental Abyss and to the Land of Fire, before the hardened shell had begun to crack. Doran is a good person. Not only is he a good person, he is also my friend. And I can't just stand by and watch this happen.

"He knows where Dad is. We have to do something," I hiss.

"We can't risk it, Ka," Sloan says gently.

"Unless you want to have a big, neon arrow pointing to you so that the rest of the Imminent Darkness can find you," Li adds.

"There's only four of them. That's one each."

"I will battle with you, my friend," Cerise interjects nobly. I sure hope that means she has a knife or something hidden in her braided hair.

"Are you going to let two girls do this alone, or are you going to help us?" I prod.

Sloan runs a hand over his face and sighs. Li rolls his eyes. I take both gestures as an affirmation that they'll help. I pull the dagger from my messenger bag and hand it Sloan. Truthfully, it's his and not mine. Besides, I have my own weapons. He clutches the glistening handle. And nods.

"Wait for my signal," I say. The figure takes Doran's forearm and holds it over the flames. A dark droplet of blood rolls out of the cut in his mocha-colored skin and falls as if in slow motion, before landing in the flames. Doran is a Fire. His blood is ripe with it. They are feeding the flames. Making a sacrifice. Maybe they finally realized the Imminent Darkness cannot be trusted, and foolishly think their silly, human sacrifices can control it. The flames shoot up into the air, turning white and creating the perfect wall. Albeit, only a temporary one. But I'll take it.

"Now!" I roar and we leap out of the shadows. First things first, I release my vines onto the figure holding Doran. They shoot out and wrap around the man's arms, pinning them to his waist, much like the kraken did to me. The man swears and Doran stumbles forward.

"Ka?" he chokes out. His face is dirty and tear-streaked.

"Hi," I say. "We need to get you out of these."

"Knife, back pocket," he says. I follow his instructions and pull a small knife, disguised as some sort of playing card. It flips open.

"You hang out with Li too much." I cut off his binds and he grins.

"Not like you're here."

I hand him back the knife, he takes it in his hand. Blood slowly drips down his forearm. "I am now."

We join the fight. Li has been left weaponless, but I'm not too worried about him. He's immortal after all. Although not invincible. He right hooks the figure holding the dagger, directly in the temple and the person stumbles back, the dagger falls out of his hand. The hood slips off. Salt and pepper hair, menacing brown eyes, and a slippery smile. Eoin. Tristen's henchman. But without Tristen, I guess he's stepped into newer roles.

He staggers forward, the eye that received the blow already swelling shut, and swings at Li who ducks. The punch lands on my shoulder and sends me backwards into Doran. Who knocks over the trash bin. Flames immediately spread to the surrounding garbage, licking and lapping. We look at each other clearly thinking the same thing: *Oh, shit.*

"Look what you've done!" yells Eoin, making a leap toward the sprawled trash bin. "My sweet!"

Li yanks Eoin backward by his hair. I slide across the ground and grab the dagger. Beside me Cerise has picked up someone twice her size and is holding them over her head like a championship fighter, as if it's nothing at all she hurls the person across the Black Bazaar. The figure hits the side of one of the metal vendors with a *clang,* then slides to the ground motionless. Apparently, turning human has not eliminated the gift of supernatural strength. That leaves one more plus Eoin. Sloan stumbles over to Cerise, Doran, and I, a hooded figure lays against one of the vendors, a pool of blood forming around his leg. I know Sloan, and it's most likely only a wound that will buy us some time, not one that will be fatal. That's not Sloan.

The fire rages on. Consuming the now empty bench, then easing up the lamp post. Some of the awnings belonging to the vendors have caught fire. This is not good. Li's voice drifts over the sound of the cackling flames.

"That's for trying to kill my best friend." Flesh hitting flesh. "That's for trying to kill my other best friend."

Flesh hitting flesh. The flames part just enough that I can see Li with Eoin in a headlock, pummeling him with blow after blow to the gut. Li has something else going for him besides his youth and immortality. Rage. Vengeance. And loyalty. He pulls a bent arm up into the air above Eoin's head. He's bent over and blood drips out of his nose and lands in the flames which jump at the sudden meeting of Fire and fire. "And this is for trying to kill *me!*" He brings an elbow down hard on the back of Eoin's head and he falls to the ground. Flames begin to lick at his cloak. Li hovers over him a moment, his chest visibly heaving. The three of us stand there a moment stunned.

Li looks up and in the glow of the fire his face is grotesque: black tribal markings that snake below the collar of his shirt, hair askew, eyes wild, mouth snarled. He looks terrifying. Cerise squeezes my arm.

"Li." It's all I say, my voice barely above a whisper. His expression softens and he shakes his head as if remembering where he is and who he is with. "It's over. Let's go."

He nods and shakes his head again, as if clearing away cobwebs. There's the sound of something cracking and popping. It won't be long before the Black Bazaar is consumed in flames, my memories along with it. We run back up the cobblestone alleyway and to the main street.

Doran looks both ways, his arm still bleeding. "This way!"

We follow him, running as fast as we can because it won't be long before the rest of the Imminent Darkness finds their broken brethren and before everyone finds the Black Bazaar up in flames. I can only hope that if there's any people left, they find a way out. Although I'm pretty sure there were no people left. No good, decent people anyways. Only the Imminent Darkness.

We run through the center of the University Complex which looks dreary and abandoned. The twin moons are high, allowing enough light with which to read the iron scrolls that welcome each student: *Divide et Impera*. Divide and conquer. Those words have a much different meaning for me now than they used to. Campus only consists of five buildings and we run out the other side and climb over the low stone wall, houses are further apart here. Concrete houses mix with stone houses and some simple wooden, cabin-like homes. This is not so much a neighborhood as a scattering of dwellings. Just past the last house is a cluster of trees. Their leaves still silvery green in the moonlight. I've never been here before. When I was young, I wasn't much for exploring. We enter the cluster of trees and immediately I feel relief as if I am somehow unseen and protected in this small, forest. If you could call it a forest. After being in the Land of Wood, I'm not sure that it counts, but it feels good nonetheless.

Our pace has slowed. Doran stops. For the first time, I notice that Cerise is holding Li's hand, her pale fingers intertwined with his darker ones. The look on his face bears no resemblance to what I saw in the Black Bazaar. His eyes are calm pools of brown and his mouth forms a serene line. What mermaid magic has Cerise worked?

"Here," Doran says.

"Where is here?" I ask. He gestures and I notice that one of the trees has an opening at its base, partially blocked from view by its root system. I give him a quizzical look, but he just shimmies beneath the roots and into the hole and disappears into the darkness. I look back at Sloan.

"Stranger things have happened."

I smile at that and shrug. Then shimmy my way behind Doran, followed by Sloan, Cerise, and then Li. We can't stand completely up, but I take one step forward and slam into Doran.

"Woah, there," he says and takes my hand, pulling me through the darkness. I grab Sloan's hand and we form a little train. We make our way downwards sliding in the dirt. Down and down we go for what seems like minutes until Doran abruptly stops. I'm about to ask him just what's going on when I realize why he stopped.

We're standing on a precipice. Below is row after row of cream-colored tents, forming a grid. They go on and on until my eyes lose focus. A soft glow encases the tents. They look warm and inviting. More importantly they look safe. Sloan peers over my shoulder and he audibly gasps at the sight. From this height I can see a few shadowy figures moving about in between the rows of tents.

"Doran," I whisper suddenly afraid that if I make my voice any louder, I'll disturb the tranquility expanding before us. "What is this place?"

He looks back at me, his hand still clasped in mine. There's a shine to his coffee-colored eyes and his long, lashes are damp.

"Home."

CHAPTER 20

Zora hands me a steaming mug of tea. I wrap my hands around it. Doran is pressed on one side of me and Sloan is on the other. We're sitting on an old trunk made of weathered wood with metal rivets. Mrs. Chatfield is out tending to the sick or the wounded, making sure everyone in this makeshift shanty town has the things that they need. That's just the type of person she is: one who keeps people safe. Li and Cerise sit on the floor, Li's back rests against my legs.

When we arrived, Doran explained, as we followed him down the wooden staircase, that this is where the people had come, fearing for their lives. Mostly the Metals, who abandoned their businesses in preference of securing their own safety. I saw some other Elementals, mostly Earths and a few Woods and Waters also walking around. The Black Bazaar had been taken over first, so it makes sense that the

Metals left so quickly. Balanced Metals are strategists. They make excellent soldiers who are both strong and calculating. However, Metal is also the Element most likely to become Unbalanced, which makes them dishonest, manipulative, and aggressive. A danger not only to others, but to themselves as well.

A couple of lanterns hang in the corners of the tent, which by tent standards, is quite large. Big enough for a card table, and a couple of chairs, as well as two cots. Before she left to check on the others, Mrs. Chatfield explained that when the colony was first settled and the physiological affects discovered, this is where the Earths resided, until eventually they were persuaded to live closer to their neighbors, abandoning the cavern in the forest for something more practical. She winked at Sloan as she added that only people up on their Xon 9 history would remember such a place. Apparently, she and Zora, as well as a few others, had been preparing the cavern for just such an occasion, creating a sort of safe house. Or in this case, more like a safe city.

Xon 9 has approximately 3,000 people…not much of an increase from the original settlement. We may have longevity, but there's also strict guidelines for population control and food rationing in order to avoid two of the major problems that plagued Old Earth. There's easily 800 tents in here. Mrs. Chatfield also explained that the cavern is very deep and that this room, spills into another, and so on for several kilometers. In order to avoid the logistics of it all, everyone brought with them what they could until they could come to some sort of consensus.

Zora hands her brother a chipped mug, and my father's watch glints in the dim light of the lanterns. Doran is my friend. I've saved him and he's saved me enough for there to no longer be a debt. Then why is it so hard to ask him about the watch? *Because what if he's dead?* A tiny voice in the back of my mind answers. Sloan squeezes my hand as if he can hear the conversation. For once, I don't mind. Still, it would be better to know.

"Doran." My voice comes out in a croak. I clear my throat. Doran looks at me sideways over the rim of his mug.

"I know what you're going to ask me, Ka. And he's fine." I feel the relief of a weight being lifted from my shoulders, making me wish I'd asked sooner. Like when we first left the Black Bazaar. "But." He glances down into his mug. "I don't know where he is."

"Then how do you know her father is fine?" Cerise asks. It doesn't come out rude sounding like it would if Li, or even I, had asked.

"He was here. And he gave me this watch, telling me that you'd know what to do with it. I asked him how I'd be able to find you. He replied that you would come to me." He looks up and smiles. "Got that part right. Then he gave me these and told me to give them to you." He reaches into his pants pocket and hands me a packet of matches with a crisp white cover. The Old Tavern and the Sea.

"Guess we really need to find that place," Sloan says looking over my shoulder at the packet with its picture of a siren.

Doran shrugs. "Sorry, but that's all I've got. After that he was gone." Doran unfastens the watch and hands it to me. I want to take it. I really do. But if my father gave it to Doran then there was a reason.

"No, you keep it." I hold my index finger that wears the ring he made for me. "Already got one."

"What does it do?" Zora asks. She's leaning against the tent opening, her slender, athletic frame cast in shadows. Only the glint of her metallic threads stand out on her dark face.

"It has a living memory. It remembers where it was last, which in this case is our family home in the Land of Earth. My ring works slightly differently, but it's the same general idea."

Doran refastens the watch onto his wrist. Zora pops her head outside of the tent opening, then back in. "It's getting late. We all should get some rest. There's a meeting tomorrow."

"Meeting?" I ask.

"Strategic meeting. We can't just sit around here and let the Imminent Darkness destroy the colony. Something needs to be done." She plucks the pack of matches of out my hand, inspecting them, then tosses the pack back to me. "This place sounds familiar. Let me sleep on it. We can talk more in the morning."

We pull blankets and pillows out of the chests, arranging them in a sort of child-like fort on the floor. I end up squeezed between Sloan and Cerise. The noise outside the tent becomes softer. Zora blows out the lanterns and through the thin cloth of the tent, I can see others doing the same. The darkness is opaque, but at the same time it doesn't feel oppressive or threatening. It feels almost warm and comforting. For the first time in a long while, I'm surrounded by people who I love and who love me back. People who want to help me and who don't blame me for the consequences that may come with that. Friends who've become my family.

. . .

Sloan's breath is slow and even to my right. I can feel his chest rise and fall against my back. In front of me I can barely make out Cerise's sharp features. I can't tell if her eyes are open or closed. All around us is stillness, except for the gentle breathing of the others.

"Ka?" Her voice is barely a whisper.

"Yes?"

"Back there, at that place."

"The Black Bazaar?"

"Yes. That one." Her breath brushes against my face in flowery scented puffs. "How did you do what you did?" I have to think about it for a second and retrace the evening's events before I realize she means my vines.

"It's the gift of Earth." That's the simplest answer.

"And you have others? Other gifts? Like your hand and forearm."

I haven't told Sloan or anyone else that everywhere my skin has turned black seems to have gone numb. I'm too ashamed to admit that I was dumb enough—or desperate enough—to use my Fire gift while in a land made of water. I should have known better from when I destroyed the Fire stone in the pool beneath the Water Building. It was catastrophic. I almost died. If Sloan hadn't been there, I probably would have.

"Yes."

"You've retrieved three other stones."

"I have." I tick them off in my mind. "Earth. Fire. And Wood." The Water stone is still nestled securely in my pocket for now.

"Then what is the gift of Wood?" Her voice is soft and there's a breathy pause between each word as if she is falling asleep.

"Sentience."

There's a long pause and for a moment I'm sure that she's fallen asleep, then softly: "I don't understand."

"I can see…things. Trees live a very long time. They watch the changes around them. From its birth as an acorn to its death as a snag…some trees live for hundreds of years."

"How does it work?"

"I'm not completely sure."

"Have you done it before?"

"Once." An image flashes in my mind. One of Li growing from mischievous child, to a man who would betray an entire army of collective consciousness to try and warn his best friend and first love that she was in danger, to a warrior with a red-haired maiden by his side. With Cerise by his side.

"Tell me."

I swallow and the sound is loudly audible between our faces. I can still feel the warmth of her breath on my cheeks. Do I dare? To see the future has never been a gift that I thought desirable.

"I can't control what I see." I tell her cautiously, but also knowing that for Cerise it most likely isn't a deterrent. She's in an unknown world in an unfamiliar body, neither of which she's had much control over.

"Tell me." Her voice is soft, but insistent.

"Give me your hand," I whisper. There's a gentle rustle as our fingers find one another's and I close mine around hers. Then, despite the blackness, I close my eyes. The visions don't come every time I touch someone. There has to be an openness on the one end, in Li's case unconsciousness, and an intention on the other end, in this case and in all cases, my intention.

Cerise is an open book. I see her in the castle tending to Tullia. She was a servant of some kind. Then I see a young human man brought forth. A gift from the kraken. He's kept in a room in one of the castle's towers, until Tullia is ready for him. Cerise is instructed to tend to him. The images come rapid fire. Blinding flashes of a life once lived. They fall in love. I can see it on their faces. In the way they touch one another. Cerise tries to save him, but Tullia is too strong and too wise. Cerise is forced to watch as Tullia consummates with the man, who is now turning into a merman. A merman with beautiful purple eyes. And black hair. *Ridge?* My stomach churns, but the images keep coming. Cerise flees as far away as she can. She makes do on her own for a while. Living simply. Then she finds me. She's curious and lonely. So she helps me. She helps me escape and then helps me save Sloan, knowing that we aren't the only ones looking to escape the Land of Water.

An image of her glancing at Li shyly. Li's radiant smile. His hands warm around her perpetually cold ones. Something shifting. The images come faster, almost too fast for me to keep up. I see a kiss and then I see a shadow, thick, black and grotesque. Li convulsing, then Cerise holding him, pressing him against her heart space. Where is the image of Li with the bow and arrow that I've already seen? What about Li's immortality? The images swirl, the colorful image of Cerise holding Li in her arms, with the black shadow, forming a swirling vortex. Then the vortex bursts in a blinding light and I see the image of Li's angular face superimposed with Cerise's pixie-like features and then they dissolve as one.

My heart is beating fast and I can feel droplets of sweat on my upper lip. I slowly let go of Cerise's hand as I try to process the confusing images. It seems like hours have passed, but in reality it's only been seconds. My pounding heart begins to slow. I swallow. Cerise reaches across the space between us and puts her cool hand onto my burning hot cheek.

"What did you see?"

What did I see exactly? I saw loyalty and betrayal. Hurt and anguish. Shame. Guilt. I saw second chances. I saw first glances. I swallow and reply hoarsely, "Love. I saw love."

CHAPTER 21

So, if I have this correct, my father was here. And then he wasn't. No one knows where Ahna is which, quite frankly, scares the bejeezus out of me. I can't shake the image of her glowing, yellow eyes out of my head. Or her angry words. Ahna and I have pretty much never fought. That was more Li's style. My heart aches to think that I've hurt her so much that she can't forgive me. That we can't somehow work it out. The list of people—and places—to find seems to grow longer.

There are two camping chairs in front of the tent. I sit and twirl the two identical packs of matches between the fingers of either hand, lost in thought. The packs aren't totally identical. One is clearly older and missing some matches. The other looks new, the white background still pristine. It contains all its matches in two neat little rows like obedient, flammable soldiers. I'd never heard of this place until a few months ago and now it seems I can't stop hearing about it. Who—or what—is there?

It's early and Mrs. Chatfield has already left. That's what she does: tends to the sick, feeds the hungry, and soothes the frightened. Wearing a cheery smile, the cobweb of her metallic threads glinting in the light, she'd set out before everyone else was awake. Except for me. It's hard to sleep when the safety of everyone you care about is in jeopardy. And your best friend is mad at you. And your father has gone missing. Again.

A girl walks past me and mumbles something. I nod in greeting. She's headed down the row to where Doran told us there's a well. I watch her retreating figure and long, blonde ponytail. My stomach lurches. Diadona? But it can't be. Her simple t-shirt is stained and there's dirt smudges on her arms and bare legs. She glances back over her shoulder at me. Blue eyes peer back at me, but there's no antagonistic spark. The beginnings of silvery-green scales line her forehead, up near her hairline. The Change incomplete. For a moment I think she recognizes me. How could she not? She made my school years a miserable blur with her constant taunting. But her eyes are blank and she turns back around, disappearing down the aisle. Do I look that different? Or am I still just that invisible?

There's a rustle behind me and Zora appears. She hands me a bowl of dry cereal and then sits down in the chair opposite me. "What happened to your hand?"

I'd reached for the bowl with my left hand, forgetting to pull down my sleeve to cover the blackened skin. I scoop up some of the cereal with my good fingers—the ones that still have feeling in them—and drop several of the crispy, round grains into my mouth.

"Freak electrical accident."

Zora smirks. "Freak is right." But it doesn't feel like a taunt coming from her like it would have from Diadona. Zora met me when I first became a Fire. We've been friends for a couple of months now. So before I can lose my courage, I ask her the questions that's bugged me since Diadona walked away.

"Have I changed, Zora?"

She takes a slow sip from a steaming mug, considering my words. She tilts her head from side to side. Then finally, she replies. "Yes."

"Good or bad?"

"Is it ever that simple?" She smiles.

"You know what I mean."

"Okay. It's like this, right? When Doran pronounced Fire, which I knew he would, he'd rather die than become an Unbalanced Water like Dad or an Unbalanced Metal like Mom. At least that's how he used to think. He was all arrogant and pissy all the time." I remember that. Doran was disrespectful during our first new initiate meeting and Tristen used physical reprimand. Not to mention the other, more questionable methods she used later. I'd seen Doran go from cocky to broken in a matter of days. "And then he came back from wherever he went with you, and he was all excited and talking about magical places, and other worlds. He was like a different person." She looks down into her mug as if it will give her answers. "It was how he was before Dad. It's like that. With you."

"I was pissy and now I'm not?" I ask confused.

She laughs. "No. When you came for your tattoo and I first met you, I liked you. You seemed nice. A bit shy, maybe. And now…when I look at you." I lean forward. *Am I still invisible?* I want to ask, but the words are caught in my throat. She looks up at me and there's something shining in her eyes. At first I don't recognize it, but then with a thump of my heart, I do: it's hope. She continues, "When I look at you, I see magical places, and faraway worlds, and a person willing to risk all she's ever known in order to learn the truth."

I don't reply because I don't know what to say. Is it true? Am I risking everything I've ever known to learn the truth? My heart speaks before my brain. Yes, because I believe the truth is out there and it will set us free, because the truth is infinitely better than any of the lies we tell ourselves. The Universe is a vast place, and it's okay to believe in magic, and it's okay to believe in things that we can't explain with our own paltry five senses. If it was all explained, what would there be left to discover? The truth can shatter your fragile reality, but when you finally put the pieces back together it can create something better. You only have to let it. My mom taught me that.

Zora reaches over and puts a reassuring hand on my arm. "You've given my brother and my family a wonderful gift, Ka. It's nice to have my brother back, even if I didn't realize how gone he really was."

I'm about to tell her that it had little to do with me, when there's a rustle behind us and Doran appears in the entrance to the tent, rubbing the sleep from his eyes.

"Did I hear my name?"

"Not unless you know anything about the Old Tavern and the Sea," I reply.

"Oh that reminds me. I think I know where I've heard of that place." Zora looks up as if she hears a sound. Sure enough a low, baritone note rings across the tent city. It seems like it will go on forever until it slowly fades away.

"What was that?"

"That's the signal that the tactical meeting is about to start. You should join us. Then I can tell you what I remember about the Old Tavern and the Sea."

. . .

It turns out that the tent city isn't just a safe haven; it's a resistance. The Elementals have come together to try and take down the Imminent Darkness. We're in an open cavern with no tents. The cavern is small and rounded, almost as if it had been dug out. There's a chalkboard on wheels at the front of the room. An older man with leathery skin stands beside the chalkboard, his metallic threads glinting in the dim light of the many lanterns lighting the room. People are sitting on the floor, some in the center forming neat little rows, others sit or stand along the outer perimeter of the room. Zora and I stand near the small, arched entryway that's been reinforced with some worn wooden boards. Her arms are crossed, but her coffee-colored eyes are curious.

Once it seems everyone is more or less settled, the man loudly clears his throat, silencing the remaining rustles and whispers. He points at the chalkboard with a stubby piece of yellow chalk. The board contains a hand-drawn map of Xon 9. It shows the University Complex in the northwest of the colony. The Underground is to the northeast. It isn't really underground of course, it's just called that because the Metals chose to call it that. At least, I think that's why it's called that. No one has ever really took the time to explain it. At the northernmost tip of the Underground is the Black Bazaar, and just southwest is the military complex. To the southeast of the University Complex is where I grew up, an outcropping of concrete houses. Near the center of the colony is where Sloan lives and further south past that are the mountains of Xon 9, containing whatever remains of the Elemental Abyss. In the north is Council Hall, just on the outskirts of the Complex. We're located south, past the perimeter, indicated by a rough drawing of some trees.

There are Xs slashed through the Black Bazaar, my neighborhood, and the University Complex. Without being told, I assume those are the areas the Imminent Darkness has infiltrated. I notice Council Hall also has an X, which makes me feel a bit better because I've spent so much time trying to convince Sloan and my father that the Leadership Council couldn't be trusted.

"Are there any new developments, for the good of the order?" The man's voice is deep and easily resonates across the room.

"There was a fire in the Black Bazaar last night!" a voice calls out. There are some gasps and some murmured whispers.

"What was the cause?" someone else calls out. More murmurs. Zora looks at me, but I purposefully avoid her eyes. What was Eoin doing? He had said he needed a sacrifice. But if Eoin is anything like Tristen, then he's not necessarily following the instructions that are coming down from the Imminent Darkness. Which means the blood sacrifice could have been for his own personal agenda. Fire for Fire. Tristen. But that's impossible. The Earth stone destroyed her. Her mutant form fractured into a million tiny pieces. Except…I'm wearing one of those pieces on my index finger. I swallow down my fear.

The Metal man raises his hands and the murmurs die down. I wonder who he is, to yield so much power. I make a mental note to ask Zora when we leave.

"The cause is irrelevant. The important thing to remember is that the Imminent Darkness is destroying our home and that we must come together to stop it."

His words make my heart beat faster. *Come together.* Even though each Elemental claimed an affiliation, studied with their fellow Elementals, and then worked with them, for the most part we've always been free to intermingle and even marry outside our Elemental. But the reasoning was that certain people are better at certain things. In order to harness those unique traits of each Element, we divided ourselves into these neat, little categories. Only those categories aren't so neat. As evidenced by Sloan who could just as easily have been a Metal. Or by Zora who could have been a Fire instead of a Metal. The list goes on.

"What about the Impossible Girl?" someone asks.

"Yes, there were reports about her being here in the colony!"

"Eh, she's just a story!"

The back of my neck grows hot.

"My father saw her! In the flesh!"

The man seems to take all this in and then raises his hand again for order. The voices fade back to hushed whispers then disappear completely.

"Real or not. We can all learn from her teachings. We are all possibilities. We are one. Therefore, we need to act as one. It is in the act of dividing ourselves that the Imminent Darkness grows stronger. When we think that we are separate entities, and not one of the same, living and breathing flesh, that is when we lash out against our fellow man."

There are some nods of ascent and mumblings of agreement.

"However, the question remains. How do we stop the Imminent Darkness and reclaim our home?"

. . .

Zora and I slip out before the meeting is finished. She tells me the man is named Zechariah. He's retired military personnel and very respected in the Underground. There was some talk about recruiting more citizens to the cause. And then there was discussion about forming an alliance with the military complex. The military is solely made up of Metals, but perhaps with enough backing from the various Elementals they could be persuaded by strength in numbers. If the Imminent Darkness is as manipulative and mysterious as they say, the stronger the need to band together.

The talks made me feel hopeful, and at the very least satisfied.

"I thought you maybe needed to hear some of that."

"That they don't think I'm real?" I ask as we walk along the rows of tents.

Zora smiles, her curls form a halo around her head. "Well, maybe not that bit. But the rest was pretty good, right?"

"Yeah, I just hope it's enough."

Her smile doesn't fade as we round the corner, heading back toward the tent. When we return, everyone's awake. Mrs. Chatfield is still gone. Doran and Sloan are sitting in the chairs Zora and I occupied earlier.

"So, now that I'm fully awake. What's the plan? Don't we have a stone to destroy?" Doran rubs his hands together like an evil villain in a kid's story.

"And a father to find."

"And a tavern to visit," adds Zora. She gestures to Doran and Sloan. "Come inside."

Li and Cerise are talking quietly, heads pushed together, when we enter and they jump apart, cheeks flushing. But I'm not surprised. Because I've already seen it in both their futures. Cerise scoots over and pats the space beside her, indicating I should sit down. Sloan settles beside me, placing a warm hand on top of my knee. My heart flutters happily at his touch. Once everyone's inside, Zora drops closed the entrance to the tent. Her secrecy surprises me. She plops down in a chair beside her brother.

"If I am following all this correctly, when you first began looking for the Elemental stones, Bina gave you a sack filled with random objects, one of which was the pack of matches from the Old Tavern and the Sea." I nod. "And then your father also gave my brother a pack of matches from the same place."

"Seems an odd coincidence," Li pipes up.

"Mom doesn't believe in coincidences," Sloan says. "If Bina put that packet of matches in there and Ka's dad had a pack too, then there's something there that she's meant to find."

"Right. The only problem is none of us have heard of this place," I say.

"Except," interjects Zora. "In the tattoo shop. Lots of different people come—came—in and out of there. One time a Water came in. He wanted a tattoo of a mermaid, not too different from the one on the matches." I pull one of the packs of matches from where I stashed them earlier, in the pocket of my cargo pants. I toss it to her. "Now, I don't know much, but when people are squirming under the needle, they sometimes have the tendency to spill their guts. He said that he was out in the lands past the colony limits, out South."

"What was he doing out there?" I interrupt. As far as I know, not many people ventured out that way, present company excluded.

Zora shakes her head. "He'd just found out his wife was taken ill. Terminal." Terminal illness is not common in our colony. We have superb medical personnel. But not every disease and illness has been accounted for over the last eight-hundred years. There are still some that we haven't found cures for. "So he was just walking and feeling rightfully miserable, when he said there it was. A small tavern, made of grey stone, vibrant green moss climbing up its walls."

"Green moss?" Li interrupts, but Cerise shushes him.

"He said there was a sign hanging. It had a mermaid on it like the one he was getting tattooed on his arm."

"What did he do?" Cerise asks, clearly curious.

"He went inside. He said there was no one else there, just some old wooden tables and some wooden barstools. Then, from seemingly out of nowhere, an old man appeared. He was wiping down the counters as if he'd been there the entire time. The old man told him to have a seat and asked what seemed to be the trouble. So, he found himself telling the old man about his terminally ill wife. The old man listened, nodding in sympathy, and even gave the man a drink on the house. But then this is where things get strange."

"As if this story wasn't strange already," Doran mumbles.

Zora cuts him a defiant glare. Doran shrinks back into his seat, defeated.

"The old man handed him a vial of shimmery, silver liquid. He told the man to give it to his wife. The man thanked him and left. When he realized he hadn't been given additional instructions besides give her the elixir, he turned and was going to go back inside to ask the old man. But the entire place was gone."

"Like disappeared"? I ask.

Zora nods. "Completely vanished."

CHAPTER 22

My boots scrape across the red earth and a breeze goosebumps the skin on the back of my neck. The twin moons are just cresting the horizon. I don't have a lot of time, but should have just enough to return to the tent city before curfew. I flip the hood of my gray hoodie over my head.

It isn't that I wanted to come alone. It just made the most sense. The man in Zora's story had been alone, and what if the tavern didn't appear unless you were alone? Besides it isn't worth it to put more people in danger for something that seems about as real as a mirage. I squeeze the small packet of matches in between my fingers. But it is real. It has to be.

Before me is nothing, but cracked earth. Behind me is the colony, glimmering as if in actuality, it's the mirage and not the other way around. Zora wasn't exactly clear on how to make this place appear.

So I continue walking into the distance and decide my best bet is to just think of what I need. I need to find my father, that's for sure. After all he's risked to be with my mother and now he's just upped and disappeared. It doesn't seem fair. And I need to destroy the Water stone. I need that part of my personality, or I am incomplete. It's like completing a puzzle two-thirds of the way and then abandoning it. Sure, you can make out the majority of the picture, but part is still missing and it is still unfinished. I am unfinished. I need those missing pieces.

Suddenly, I notice a shimmer in front of me. If you weren't looking for it, you'd barely notice. It's several yards in front of me, and it's as if the air is simply…different. The shimmering stops and once again I see the barren, red landscape before me. And then again, it's shimmering and I can see the faint outline of a stone building. And just as fast as it tried to appear, it's gone again. And then it's back. This time I can see and smell the green moss creeping up its walls and the weathered sign hanging above the wooden door. I look at the matches in my hand. The sirens are identical. The shimmering stops and the place seems to have gained some sort of solidity. That is, if magic could become solid.

I step closer and run my hands along the waist high stone wall that's appeared. The stones are smooth and cool to the touch. They feel as real as they look. I inch through the walkway and reach the wooden door. Do I just walk in? Knock? Before I can make up my mind the door slowly creaks open. A sweet, musty smell beckons me inside. I step into the dim light of the tavern. The door closes softly behind me.

The old man isn't here yet, so I take a minute to take it all in. It's just as Zora described. There's a few scratched, wooden high-top tables and some chairs. The windows are glass block, but the light that filters in is golden-white, instead of the usual pink. I run my fingers lightly over the bar top which is some kind of smooth, black stone with white lines in it. The edge of the counter is weathered wood that appears to be made silken from the many hands that have come to touch it. There are seven leather topped stools in front of the bar, so I decide to sit and wait.

On the counter is a crystal bowl filled with packets of matches, identical to the other two I already have. There are rows of glass bottles behind the bar. I spin around on the barstool. There are felt banners on the walls, not unlike the ones in Tullia's castle. Each a different color: emerald, sapphire, onyx, ruby, and topaz. The Elemental symbols are white and faded, but if you look carefully, you can still make them out.

A voice clears its throat behind me. I spin back around to face the bar and the old man is there, a rag in his hand, polishing the fine black stone.

"What can I get for you, Miss?" he asks. His voice has a thick accent that I don't recognize. His face is tanned and weathered. He wears an old-fashioned newsboy style cap on his head and tufts of white hair puff out either side. A bushy white mustache hides his upper lip. Bushy white eyebrows are raised up questioningly, hovering above pale gray eyes. They seem kind. The old man and the tavern.

I dig into my pocket and pull out the Water stone and place it gently on the bar top. The opalescence contrasting against the polished, black stone.

"Ah," he says nodding. He picks up the Water stone. "It has been a while since I've seen such magic. Ancient stuff this is."

"And this isn't?" I ask, gesturing at the disappearing and reappearing tavern.

"Oh dear me, no. Of course this place is magical. In fact, it's magically required per the person who needs it and is pure of heart. But this type of magic is much older than mine." He holds up the stone which shines a rainbow into the air between us.

"What do you mean *pure of heart?*"

"We don't just appear to any old person who asks."

"Who's we?"

"Me and the tavern, of course." He speaks of it as if the building is alive. And who am I to judge? For all that I know, it *is* alive.

"Can you help me destroy the stone?" I ask.

He quirks an eyebrow and his smile is teasing. He grabs a glass tumbler from behind the bar and flips it in the air before catching it again, then sets it on top of the counter in front of me. He picks up the Water stone and drops it into the glass. The Water stone hits the tumbler's bottom with a delicate *clink*. With a flourish, he pulls a pack of matches from the glass dish, taking a match and striking it against the sandpaper strip. The match ignites and he grins at me over the flame. If this place is magic, then perhaps this old man is the magician. He drops the match into the glass and there's the sound of a small explosion. A burst of brilliant rainbow colors fills the glass and a puff of white smoke rises up. The colors coalesce into a beautiful swirl before dissipating into the air between us. The man takes the tumbler and turns it over so the opening is in his palm, fine pearly grains of sand slip through his fingers and onto the black counter top.

"Done," he smiles. I drag my fingers through the crushed pearls. But I don't feel any different. Sometimes the traits don't come rushing back all at once. Sometimes I don't even realize that they've returned until I call upon them. *Resilience. Patience. Turbulence. Power.* Remember Water can both give and take away life. I find myself wondering what the gift of Water could be, not knowing that I'm about to find out.

"You have one more concern that you need help with."

It's a statement not a question. The old man dusts the pearlescent powder off the counter and back into the tumbler before placing it beneath the bar top.

I nod. "I do. My father."

"Your father"?

"Yes. He's gone missing. I need to find him. All he left behind was this. And a watch." I place one of the packs of matches on the counter. The man picks it up and turns it in his hand, a faraway expression appears in his eyes. Then he blinks and sets the packet back on the counter.

"Nope, never seen him." The man's face shimmers as he says the words and my gut wrenches in confusion. Is the magic fading? And then a knowing settles into my stomach.

"You're lying!"

"Yes. Yes, indeed I am."

"But how did I know that?"

"Just as the waters run clear with the truth, so too are the waters muddied when pooled with lies."

When the man had lied, his face had appeared to shimmer, a slight distortion overcoming his features. A sort of softening or blurring. But when he told the truth, his features sharpened back to normal. *Just as the waters run clear with the truth, so too are the waters muddied when pooled with lies.*

"My gift." Of all the things Tullia would gift to me, it's the ability to see the truth. That's ironic.

"And to be honest with you, I do remember your father. He was a very kind, Wood Elemental. Was quite worried about his daughter. That would be you then." Again a statement not a question. No distortion this time. He's telling the truth.

"Yes."

"If I remember correctly, I was to tell you to check your messages."

"My messages, but I don't have any—" And that's when I remember the sleek, silver tube in my pants pocket. I pull it out. The light is still flashing green. I look up to thank the old man, but the building that was surrounding me moments ago has already faded and disappeared. I'm left standing alone in the landscape just outside the colony, a blinking message tube in my fist.

Vanished.

. . .

My father had obviously been to the tent city. He'd seen Doran and given him his watch. Knowing Doran, maybe Dad figured he'd need to make an escape at some point. Doran has almost as uncanny a talent as myself for ending up in compromised situations. But that was Dad's only way home. Why would he forfeit his one way home? Somehow I've ended up with more questions than answers. I look at the message tube clenched in my fist. It's still flashing green.

I slide the button on the side of the tube forward. A green light emits from the end, much like a flashlight. A pixelated image of my father's face appears in the air in front of me.

"Kata. Good girl. I knew that you would find this tube when you came looking for me. There was a message waiting for me from the Council of Leaders." There's a long pause and my heart sinks. Please tell me he didn't go to them. The Council shouldn't be trusted. *Cannot* be trusted. "It was urgent. Please understand." His voice catches in his throat and he takes a second to compose himself. His eyes are pleading as if he can see me standing on the other end of the hologram. *But that's not how they work*, I remind myself. "I'll be home as soon as I can. The watch is in good hands. I love you." The green triangle in front of me collapses in on itself and then disappears. The blinking light now gone replaced with a steady red light. I pocket the tube.

I don't know if my new Water gift works on holograms, but he appeared to be telling the truth. But what could be so important that he'd risk his own life? Did the Leadership Council want to make a bargain? Or maybe they'd finally seen the truth about what was going on around them. My father had been a liege for almost twenty-years, but that didn't stop him from being kidnapped from practically right under their noses. And what about my mother?

My head's a storm of thoughts which is why I don't notice the person standing in front of me until it's too late. I'm in a deserted no-man's land all by myself. There's no one else to help me. Or to hear me.

I shouldn't be afraid.

But I am.

"Hello, Ahna."

CHAPTER 23

The girl who stands before me is named Ahna. She even looks like her. Kind of. Her caramel-colored skin is smudged with red dirt and her usual black braid is absent. Instead her hair is a snarl of tangles. She has deep, dark circles beneath her eyes, and while her eyes are their familiar brown color, they dart around like a wild animal's.

Her chapped lips form a snarl. "Kata." The voice sounds as though it is coming from someone—somewhere—else entirely, not from the petite form before me. She clenches and unclenches her fists and takes a step toward me, but it's a jerky, unnatural movement.

One time, the Imminent Darkness showed me just what it could do. Morphing from one familiar face into the next with seemingly little effort. It can change faces or bodies. It can possess any form. Human, or animal. Almost anything. It just manipulates the energetic fields around it.

I pretend to not notice all the changes. Maybe it's naïve of me. But I *want* this to be Ahna. My Ahna. And I want her to not be mad at me so badly, that I'm willing to play along. If even for a moment. Even if every cell of my body tells me to turn and run back to the tent city as fast as I can.

"Are you still angry with me?" I ask carefully. I left my messenger bag with Sloan. It's just me and my empty message tube. And my Elemental powers. I only hope that it's enough.

"You care for no one but yourself."

It's not even an accusation, it's a statement of fact. At least a fact that she believes. And I wonder how it is that the Imminent Darkness affects the mind. Yes, it can morph into anyone, but what else can it do? The brain and nervous system are all electrical impulses. All energy. What happens if it goes—stays—inside your mind? Do your memories leave? Are you no longer you?

"You know that's not true," I reply, trying to keep my voice as steady as possible, choosing my words cautiously.

"Don't lie to me!" she cries and her face contorts in anguish. What has been done to her? Worse, is it still being done to her? Can I even help?

She continues, "You almost got Li killed twice. All you care about are those stupid stones, while here everything we have loved and known is being destroyed." Her voice is hollow sounding, but the words sound like something Ahna would say. Even if they're words that I don't want to hear. "At first I thought that you could change things. But-but you can't."

Her eyes are cast downward, but there's no ignoring the slight shimmer of her face. The water clouds. She's lying. She *does* think I can change things. But why is she lying? She looks up at me again. Her face twists as if she's in physical pain. "It's…much stronger than you realize."

Her eyes roll back into her head and she sinks to the ground like a rag doll. I dash to her side and lift her shoulders, cradling her head in the crook of my elbow.

"Ahna. Ahna, can you hear me? You know that's not true. You believe in me. Otherwise, you wouldn't have come. Tell me. What is it that you're fighting? I can help you. Please. Let me try to help you." I feel the sting of tears. What's happening? Her breath is slow and ragged. A tiny droplet of blood slips from the corner of her mouth.

My brain rapidly tries to put together the pieces of what's happening. The last time I saw Ahna was in a dream. She had yellow eyes. But just now…she sort of seemed like herself. I rack my brain for anything I know about energy. Unfortunately, I was a horrible student and I'm drawing blanks. The only thing I can remember is that energy can neither be created nor destroyed. I don't even know what that means. Ahna would know. She was the smart one! She was the excellent student. Neither created. Nor destroyed. The Imminent Darkness cannot be destroyed because it was never created. But what does that even mean?

I scoop her up and struggle to my feet. She feels as light as air, like her body's been drained of all its blood and organs, and replaced with nothing but air. Like she's an empty shell of my best friend. I begin walking faster and then break into a jog. Heading back to the forest and the tent city. Mrs. Chatfield can help her. Someone has to be able to help her. Ahna takes a shuddering breath in my arms and a puff of air escapes her dried lips. It smells like sulfur and I press my lips together to stop myself from retching.

The twin moons are almost completely risen. I hurry, Ahna pressed to my chest. I'm about to step into the forest when I have a crippling thought. What if it's a trap? The Imminent Darkness has obviously gotten to her. Unlike people, my dreams don't lie. I know this is Ahna and not just a replica, not simply a form the Imminent Darkness is masquerading as. But what if it's somehow inside her mind? Eating away at her? If I take her into the tent city, I will be putting everyone in danger. And the loss of life will be even greater.

I can't do it.

I stop at the edge of the forest and find a cluster of trees that have piles of leaves and sticks covering their roots. I kick aside some of the foliage and then gently settle Ahna down on top of the pile. Her breath is still slow and shallow, almost non-existent. I squirm out of my hoodie and use it as a blanket to cover her up. If someone just walked by at first glance, they'd never notice her. She's so thin and fragile, that there isn't even much to notice. I can't shake the guilt of leaving her here when she's so clearly dying. One life versus many. A friend versus strangers. I swallow back my tears. It isn't fair that I have to make this decision. None of this is fair. I didn't ask for this.

I put my hand gently on her shoulder, feeling the bones jutting through my sweatshirt. "I'll be back, Ahna. I'm going to get help."

Her eyes flutter, long black lashes against her gaunt, dirt-smudged cheek. "Hurry. I don't have much time." She coughs and more blood splatters out of her mouth. "It knows."

No shimmer. No lies. But what does it know? More importantly how does it know? I press a fist to my mouth. *Oh, Ahna, what has happened to you?* I stand up, squashing the guilt that rises up like bile in my throat. I glance back one last time. Ahna's eyes have slid closed. The rise of her chest is barely perceptible. I close my eyes and then I run as hard as I can back to the tent city.

. . .

I'm half afraid that when we return that her body will have disappeared. My sense of what's real and what's not is beginning to get mixed up. Ahna is the Imminent Darkness. Not real. Ahna is dying. Real. She thinks I can't save them. Not real. I don't know if I can save her. Real.

Ahna is still where I left her, resting against a thick-barked tree, covered in a blanket of leaves and my sweatshirt. Her face is pale and the dried blood near her lip is still there. Li instinctively darts toward her, but I stick a protective arm out.

"We don't know what's causing it." I momentarily forget that he's immortal. But it's for the best since he doesn't know that he is.

"She's my twin," he growls, but he doesn't try to push past my arm.

Mrs. Chatfield snaps on a white mask that covers her nose and mouth. Out of her apron pocket she pulls a pair of clear goggles which she places over her eyes before snapping on latex gloves. I told her about the coughing blood. I wipe my hands on my pants nervously, my palms clammy. Sloan and the others stayed behind. Mrs. Chatfield said that until she knew what we were dealing with she couldn't run the risk of others getting injured or infected. It was risky enough that I'd encountered it and then came back to the tent city. I could have unknowingly put others at risk. But what choice did I have?

Mrs. Chatfield carefully kneels in the dried leaves surrounding Ahna, bracing herself against the trunk of the tree. She pulls a device out of another apron pocket and presses it to Ahna's forehead. Ahna groans.

"I'm here, Sis." Li's voice is weak and frightened. I wrap my other arm around him so that I'm sort of hugging him from behind. The last thing I need is for him to be broken again when he's only just begun to heal. I couldn't handle my other best friend turning on me too. As if reading my mind, Li places a hand over mine which are both clasped near his heart. "It's not your fault, Ka. I should have paid more attention, when she began disappearing and sometimes not coming home. I should have protected her."

The device beeps and Mrs. Chatfield inspects it with a frown. "Her temperature is one-hundred-and-four. But not a drop of sweat."

"That's impossible, isn't it?" I ask.

"It's peculiar is what it is. Her pulse is fifty-four. That's awfully slow. Too slow." She drops the device back into her pocket then pulls a penlight out. She tenderly pulls back one of Ahna's eyelids and I feel Li tense at the sight of Ahna's rolled back jaundiced eyes. Mrs. Chatfield shines the light in first one eye then the other. "Something isn't right."

"Have you seen this before?" Li asks, his desperation evident in his voice.

"No. I don't think I have." Mrs. Chatfield looks up at us, a hand resting lightly on Ahna's shoulder.

"It's the Imminent Darkness isn't it? It's done something to her. It's drained her energy or…or…" I say, but I'm grasping at straws because I can't think of anything else. It's like my brain has freaked out and turned itself off. Everything is a jumble inside my mind. She was fine only a few days ago. How did this happen?

"We'll take her back with us right?" Li asks.

Mrs. Chatfield shakes her head. "I can't risk it. There are hundreds of people down there." She gestures at Ahna's body which has gone very still. "Without knowing what this is…you have to think of the others." She closes her eyes. I wonder if she's thinking about Doran's dad.

"But she's my sister," Li whispers.

"I know. And I know that she's very important to both you and Ka. But, I just can't put hundreds of lives in jeopardy because of one girl."

"She'll die." I point out. "We can't just leave her here. Maybe we should take her to the hospital. Maybe they can help her."

Mrs. Chatfield shakes her head. "I think that it may be too la—"

Her voice is cut off by the faint sound of buzzing. She stops midsentence, tilting her head to better listen. Xon 9 isn't a place full of wildlife and animas. Any animals that inhabit the planet were brought her by the original colonists all those years ago, and are used primarily as a food source. There are no domesticated animals. There are no bugs. At least none that I've ever seen. Granted, I've never even seen this forest before.

We look at each other confused, unable to pinpoint where the sound is coming from. I look at the canopy of leaves above us. There isn't anything except tree tops, red sky and the now fully risen twin moons, flanking the red sun, peering down at us. Mrs. Chatfield stands up, head cocked as she listens. The buzzing grows louder. She takes a step back.

"It's coming from the girl," she says. Another step back.

"No. That's impossible." But I'm quickly proven wrong.

The tiniest of black dots flies out of Ahna's right ear. I wouldn't have noticed if not for the light of the moons, illuminating half her face. The other half rests in shadow, her chin drooped between her chest and shoulder. I nudge Li. He nods, too afraid to move. He saw it too.

The little dot dips and swirls before landing on a small, silver leaf. Mrs. Chatfield leans over and inspects it.

"It's some sort of bug."

"How is that possible?" Li asks at the same time that I ask, "Is it from the animal storage facilities?"

Mrs. Chatfield picks up one of the sticks and pokes at the little black dot.

"I think it's dead," she says.

"But the buzzing hasn't stopped," Li points out. And he's right. It hasn't. If anything the sound has increased to a steady hum.

Another little black dot crawls out from beneath Ahna's left eyelid. It slides down her cheek before taking off in a haphazard flight, before alley-ooping and landing lifeless on the ground.

"Ka…"

Mrs. Chatfield is back on her feet, ushering us away, wrapping her big arms around both of us as if her mere presence could somehow protect us. The buzzing grows louder, the hum fills my ears until I can no longer even hear my own thoughts. Li claps his hands over his own ears.

"Ka, make it stop!" He sounds like a frightened child. Helpless and scared.

"I don't know what it is!" I reply. Louder and louder until it reaches a crescendo. I watch in horror as Ahna's body begins to shake. It begins with a convulsion of her stomach and moves up to her chest and shoulders. Her arms begin to flail. Then for one horrible moment, her eyes fly open, darting around wildly, before growing round in her gaunt face.

"Sis!" Li cries, reaching out to her. But this is not Ahna. Ahna is no longer here. I realize too late that Ahna is gone. Dead.

"Look away, children!" Mrs. Chatfield orders, but she's too late.

Ahna's head begins thrashing wildly, back and forth, back and forth, faster and faster until her facial features have become a blur of brown and black. Then just as suddenly, she stops. She stares at us with blank, lifeless eyes. Slowly, her jaw slackens and her mouth slides open. As if her entire jaw has become unhinged. Her eyes roll back into her head and her entire body goes still. One tiny black dot skitters out her mouth pausing near the corner of dried blood.

And then another flutters out and lands on her chin. And then another lands on one of her eyelids. More and more dots appear. Little, black bugs flying out of her mouth until her body suddenly seizes. Heaves. I clasp my hands over my ears at the deafening hum that emits from Ahna's body. I want to look away. Know that I should look away. But I can't. Ahna's mouth drops open even further, unnaturally widening with the sickening snap of her jaw. Then hundreds of little back dots come pouring out of her mouth all at once. A swarm.

They cover her face and her shoulders, down her throat and her chest moving all at once as if they are of one mind and one body.

"What the hell is that?" Li's voice cracks on the last word and is swallowed up by the deafening hum.

The tiny bugs move as one, lifting off Ahna's body as a singular, giant black mass. They hover in the air. Buzzing. Buzzing. Buzzing. And then all at once they rise up and fly away. They exit the forest and head north in the direction of the colony. Leaving Ahna's broken body behind without a second thought. Is this the Imminent Darkness? No, there are too many. The Imminent Darkness is one. Singular. But clearly it's the ID's work. But how?

Mrs. Chatfield is the first to find herself. "We must go back. We have to tell the others."

"It's the Imminent Darkness." I say. I take a step toward Ahna's lifeless body. Sweet, sweet Ahna. I close my eyes. Our last words to each other were not that of best friends.

"We have to go back now. Those remaining in the colony must be alerted."

"What is it? What were those things" Li asks.

This time Mrs. Chatfield doesn't stop him as he moves toward Ahna's body. I don't stop him either. He squats down beside his dead twin's body and slides her eyelids closed. He brushes a finger gently over her cheek. "I'll come back, Sis. Ka, Sloan, and I. We'll come back. And we'll give you a proper burial." He moves some of the leaves to cover what's left of Ahna's ravaged body.

"Those things…it's…centuries ago on Old Earth there was something called the Bubonic Plague. It was carried by a tick, which is a very small black bug." Mrs. Chatfield stands, puffing her chest out, eyes glassy. "Given the appearance of your sister and what we all just witnessed, I would say that somehow the Imminent Darkness used your twin as an incubator."

"An incubator?" Li asks standing up and casting a solemn glance back down at Ahna.

"An incubator for those bugs, which I suspect carry some sort of disease."

"It wasn't those bugs that killed Ahna. She was already dead," I point out, trying to make sense of this.

"Yes, but whatever those bugs are carrying inside them is

deadly," Mrs. Chatfield replies.

"But they're headed toward the colony. There were hundreds of those things," I say, unable to hide the panic from rising in my voice.

My father is still somewhere in the colony. So is Li's mother and his father. All of our friends. Anyone who isn't already in the tent city. Bina and Sloan's dad, Finn. Sloan's sister.

Li's face darkens into a dangerous mix of sorrow and anger.

"Everyone could die."

CHAPTER 24

The dirt is surprisingly soft. Li insisted that he wanted to do it himself. But Li, Sloan, and I all take turns, spearing the earth with the tip of the shovel, digging into its softness. This is what she would have wanted I tell myself. She would have wanted to be buried in the earth. She was an Earth. Because of sanitation and space, we don't have graveyards like on Old Earth. We cremate our dead and it's up to the families to decide how to celebrate and mourn the life of the deceased. I've never lost anyone that was like family to me. My father's parents died before I was born and, well, Kaj and Ratayun are immortal. So there's that.

A pile of dirt has formed beside the hole that is now at least a meter deep. It's taken the majority of the night. Mrs. Chatfield was understanding about it. She handed us two shovels and said she would tell Zechariah about the swarm. A trickle of sweat runs down my spine. How has this happened? How has it come to this? Thousands of people are at risk of experiencing a fate similar to this. Even the ones who think the Imminent Darkness is on their side. Something that ancient and that evil isn't on anyone's side.

I was told it's all about balance. But I'm only one person. Although, now Li is immortal too, so I guess that makes two of us. Well, one and a half of us. How do the deaths of thousands equate to that? How is that balance?

Li stands in the hole, tossing up piles of dirt. Sweat drips down his face. Sloan pushes his hair back and gives me a grim look. I toss my shovel to the ground for now and kneel beside Ahna. I did my best to clean her up, using a wet rag to clean the dirt and blood from her face. I ran my fingers through her hair and made it into as neat a braid as I could, all the while reminding myself that my best friend was gone. There would be no more late night discussions about Sloan. No more friendly chastising about my indecision. Ahna was one of the first people I went to for help when I found out the legend was real, and that I was the Impossible Girl. She helped me find out who I was and gave me the courage to confront my mom about my true identity. Sweet, reliable Ahna. Until, I gave her one too many reasons to not trust me. But something nags at me.

When exactly did the Imminent Darkness get hold of her? We were outside the military complex. The Imminent Darkness had hold of Li...Ahna was there. We used my memory ring to get to the Land of Earth. That's when Ahna grew angry with me. While we were at the castle. What if whatever had infected her happened *before* we traveled to safety? What if all this time it wasn't really her angry with me, but the Imminent Darkness and its dark magic? A tiny, black dot harvesting and incubating inside her, using her body as a weapon. I remember the shimmer of her face as she told me I couldn't do it, that I would never win. She was lying. My head spins and I feel nauseous. If I had known I could have done something. We could have saved her.

"Ka?" Sloan's voice is soft and he puts a warm hand on my shoulder. I look up into his sad, emerald eyes. I stand up and wrap my arms around his waist. The words are on the cusp of my lips right as Li calls up.

"Okay, Sloan. Bring her down!"

Sloan gives me a concerned look that clearly says we'll be discussing this later. I don't know if he's been into my thoughts or not. My mind is a jumbled mess and it's easier for him to slip into my mind when I'm feeling vulnerable. Not that he'd take advantage. Just sometimes I think he accidentally sees my thoughts, when we're both being completely open it's like our brains become soft and pliable. Except, for now, the intrusion still remains one-sided.

Ever-so-gently, Sloan scoops up Ahna's body. Her arms hang limply. My stomach seizes. Mr. and Mrs. Sollomon don't even know that their only daughter is dead. Li reaches up and takes his sister, whose body weighs almost nothing. Just a shell empty of all the vibrancy it once contained. Sloan lowers himself into the hole, sliding down the last part, then turns and reaches for me. I squat down and lean forward, allowing his arms to wrap around my waist as he lowers me to the ground.

Li lays Ahna carefully down. He folds her hands over her stomach. I pull some silvery leaves from the pocket of my hoodie. It was the best I could do. I wish I could have gone and brought back flowers from the Land of Earth. Ahna would have loved that. But there's no time. We're running out of it. I sprinkle the leaves around her body so that they form a ring around her. She looks like she could be sleeping. Like any minute she'll wake up and I can tell her that I'm sorry. I'm sorry that I almost got Li killed twice. And I'm sorry that our last words were angry ones. Mostly, I'm sorry I couldn't make a difference. I couldn't help her until it was too late.

Li kneels beside her body, a hand cupped gingerly over hers. A tear slides down his dirty cheek, leaving a streak of tanned skin. I choke back a sob and bury my face in Sloan's shoulder which shudders beneath me. Li stands and reaches for my hand. I pull away from Sloan and grasp his fingers. Then grasp Sloan's hand with my free one. He reaches across Ahna's body and Li clasps his hand. We form a ring around her, the only sound is our ragged breaths.

"I-I…" Li's face twists in anguish and he lets out a choked sob.

Sloan clears his throat carefully, tears slowly sliding down his cheeks and dripping from his chin to his dirt-stained t-shirt. "Ahna was a lovely young woman. It was an honor to have her in my classes. She was an exceptional student and, later, an exceptional friend." He glances at me and I nod.

"Ahna was smart and funny. Always kind and willing to be there for me, no questions asked. Ahna loved me before I became the

Impossible Girl. She loved me when I was still just Ka. And nothing else." I pause remembering the soft, shimmer of her features. The lie. "And she believed in me," I whisper.

Li takes a deep breath, his chest puffing with the effort. "And she was an extraordinary sister. The best sister. She was only older by a minute, but she never let me forget it. Always looking out for me and making sure I was being my best self. Her love for me—for all of us—" He looks over her body at me, brown eyes resolute. "Was unconditional. No matter what."

"Always," Sloan adds.

"Forever," I mumble suddenly overcome with another wave of grief. My shoulders shake as we finally drop hands. I lean down and kiss Ahna's cold cheek, smelling the metallic scent of blood and the soapy water from the rag, mixed with the moist sent of earth. Sloan helps me back up out of the hole and then climbs out behind me, leaving Li alone with his sister—for the last time. The sobs rack through me and Sloan just holds me pressed against his chest.

This could have been different. We could have been different. I just needed time. It's never enough. Li pulls himself up out of the hole and silently hands Sloan one of the shovels. Sloan carefully accepts it, untangling my knuckles from his shirt. I sit on the ground, my knees pulled up to my chest, and arms wrapped around myself, watching as they shovel the pile of fresh dirt back into the hole.

My tears are hot on my face. The sound of the earth hitting the bottom of Ahna's grave with such finality. My stomach churns and I feel a familiar sensation trickling through my veins burning me up from the inside out. A tear rolls to my chin and hangs, suspended at my jawline. My skin burns. The teardrop sizzles and evaporates to nothing before it has a chance to fall.

I did not do this.

The Imminent Darkness did this.

And I will kill it.

CHAPTER 25

"Are you sure it's dead?" Cerise asks peering at the tiny black dot. She's hovering beneath the table so that only her forehead and hazel eyes appear above the surface.

Zechariah takes a long metal stick, like a pointer a teacher would use, and pokes at the dot that lies on a paper towel in the center of the table. Nothing happens.

"Definitely dead," says Doran.

"Tell me again what happened, Chanice." Zechariah runs a hand down his face as if he's exhausted. His brown eyes are so dark, they are almost black, but they convey a lot of worry over the night's turn of events.

"The girl—"

"Ahna," Li and I correct at the same time. Mrs. Chatfield bows her head in apology.

"Ahna was found by Ka and brought to the forest. When Ka found her she appeared agitated and sick. She then collapsed. Luckily, Ka was smart enough to realize it could possibly be a trick, even though she is friends with the girl. Either way, I went to take a look. She was barely alive. Low pulse. High fever. And then, well, and then a swarm of these bugs came up and out of her mouth and flew off toward the colony." Mrs. Chatfield doesn't add the part about Ahna's death. It's obvious. But also unnecessary.

At first Zechariah thought we should have done an autopsy instead of burying her, but Mrs. Chatfield was quick to point out that the contagion that infected Ahna could still be alive inside her. Which then raises the question of Li, Sloan, and me. We could be contagious. Can we catch whatever made Ahna sick from merely touching her? Was one of us bit and just doesn't know it yet?

Zechariah points the metal stick at me. "You there. Ka was it?" I nod still in shock. *Ahna is gone.* "You were exposed the longest. Perhaps I should have one of the scientists take you up to the labs and run some tests."

"Me?" I squeak.

"You can't do that! She's the..." But Doran's voice just trails off as Zora cuts him a withering glare.

"Zechariah, if the child was exposed surely the damage would have already been done. The answers lie inside the insect. It is what should be dissected and studied. How did it get inside her? Where did it come from? How does it infect its victims and worse what happens once it does?"

"We don't have enough time," I groan. "Those tests could take days or weeks. What if people in the rest of the colony are already infected?"

"She has a point," Sloan says putting a hand on my shoulder. "My sister works in the military complex. You can give us the insect. And they can run the needed tests. As you already know, the complex has very advanced technology when it comes to bio warfare."

Zechariah sighs and if sighs could talk I am sure this one would say that he's tired. Tired of being the one everyone goes to for help. Tired of the one making the big decisions. Just plain tired.

"I suppose you're right. We scarcely have any lab equipment down here. And going to the Earth Building labs would also be risky, what, with those hooligans running around like they own the place." He reaches into a box nestled beneath the table and pulls out a pair of tweezers and a corked test tube.

He uncorks it and uses the tweezers to pick up the insect. He drops it in and it lands on its back, little legs suspended in the air, then corks it. He sets the tweezers down on the table and Cerise's face immediately uncreases. He hands the test tube to Sloan, who slips it into the pocket of his hoodie.

"We're going to have to do something soon, Chanice. This can't go on." Zechariah plops down onto one of the stools surrounding the table, his shoulders sagging with the weight of responsibility.

"We need to align with the military. We're on the same side," Mrs. Chatfield replies.

"But how can we be sure? If this Imminent Darkness has

infiltrated our military...then..." He doesn't have to go on to say that it would be a lost cause. If the Imminent Darkness has hold of the military, then it's over. Every Balanced Metal is part of the military. Metal is the strongest Element. A balanced Metal is not only physically strong, but mentally as well. It's the most invasive Element and takes a lot of power to control it. I can't imagine the Imminent Darkness breaking through that. What had Sloan's father said? The ID is primitive and irrational, seeking instant gratification and pleasure. Getting inside the mind of a Metal, I would think, is probably the opposite of pleasurable.

"Then we just won't think about that," Mrs. Chatfield says, patting his hand. She turns to me. "Ka, I want you and Sloan to go to the military complex. See if his sister can run those tests. Try and return by sun down. It's safer that way. Besides, the military needs to know the answers more than we do. As far as we know they're the ones who are going to be affected the most."

"I'm going too. She was my sister." Li's jaw is rigid and his eyes unfocused. I glance at Sloan and he gives a small shrug.

"Well, if Li's going, then I'm going too." Cerise says sitting up and throwing her shoulders back.

I run my fingers along my forehead. This is a bad idea.

We head out of the cavern, leaving behind the others and head back to the tent so I can grab my messenger bag. When I emerge, there are four people instead of three waiting for me.

"Like, I'm gonna let you guys go and have all the fun. My ribs are finally healed. It's bad enough I missed everything else." Doran gives me an impish smile.

I'm happy for the support, this ragtag group of friends. A mermaid turned human, a drained Fire, a waterless Water who acts as my protector, and…a Doran.

"It's dangerous," I say even though I know it won't deter any of them.

"Just the way I like it," Doran smirks.

"More dangerous than Tullia?" Cerise asks and I remember the vision of Cerise as she was forced to watch Ridge being cursed.

"The Imminent Darkness is stronger than Tullia," I reply. "More dangerous than all the Elemental goddesses put together."

Cerise shudders. "I didn't think there was something more evil than the Water Queen."

"You have no idea," I say. "Are you sure you want to come?" I think of how quickly Cerise sacrificed her mermaid-hood for Sloan. Okay, maybe not just for Sloan, but to become human. She didn't even think twice. I don't want to be the one who causes her new life to be short-lived.

She glances at Li, twisting the tail of her frayed braid in between her pale fingers. "Yes. I want to help. If this is my new home, then I want to help save it."

I shrug. There isn't much arguing that.

"Here, you'll need this." Li tosses something toward me and I catch it in my fist. A silver bracelet. A cloaking cuff. I look at him quizzically. "Sloan's sister hates you."

"Hate's a strong word," I mumble slipping the cuff over my

wrist. With the press of a button I'll be rendered invisible.

"No," Sloan smiles. "I'm pretty sure she hates you. If I recall correctly, the last time I—we—saw her she said that you will be the death of me."

How could I forget? Michaela practically wants my head on a silver platter. She doesn't believe in the Impossible Girl, that I'm real flesh and blood, despite the truth in front of her face. All she knows is I was involved in an incident with Tristen's army of Fire and that I freed a bunch of prisoners who were secretly being kept beneath Council Hall. To Michaela, my motives are both suspicious and questionable. Worse, she doesn't want her brother to have anything to do with me. I can't completely blame her. Her own father was imprisoned for speaking out against the Leadership Council, and her mother practically had her MindCleansed because of her Sight. Because of her visions of the Impossible Girl. Because of me. It nearly killed her. We reach the forest, the warm breeze caressing my face.

Sloan must sense my anxiety because he takes my hand in his and gives it a reassuring squeeze. Once, he told me that Michaela was the odd one out in the family. Even though Sloan pronounced Water and everyone else was a Metal, Michaela was the family member lacking any kind of gifts. Bina has the Sight and can dream walk. Sloan can dip into my thoughts and travel to my dreams. And Finn...now that I think about it, I'm not sure what Finn can do. Sloan leans into my shoulder.

"He's a mastermind."

"You did it again." I scowl up at him.

"I'm sorry, but you're an open book right now. I don't always do it on purpose, sometimes you're so open it's like your thoughts are made of sand and I can just sink right in."

I decide that this offense can slide. I have too much on my mind anyways to worry about letting Sloan see some of my thoughts. Luckily, nothing embarrassing has been on my mind lately. "What do you mean mastermind?"

"He's like a human computer. He can see something once and remember it. Research, specific dates, random factoids, faces. Well, used to be able to remember faces." Sloan frowns. When Finn was imprisoned he was blinded to remind him of his wrongdoing. How naïve I'd been to think that physical reprimand was a thing of the past. Just like with Doran and Everly.

"That's amazing," I say as we reach the forest's edge. Doran, Li, and Cerise's footsteps come to a stop behind us. "No wonder the Council considered him a threat."

"Truthfully, they have no idea." He doesn't elaborate, just stares off into the distance and the glowing lights of the rest of the colony. "If you didn't know that almost a third of the people had fled to the tent city, from a distance it looks the same as always. Except everything is different now. And it will never be the same."

Our hands are still clasped together and I can feel his heartbeat through the pulse in his wrist. "Maybe it's not the same," I concede. "But maybe we can make it better."

He smiles down at me and pulls me forward out of the forest and into the open space just outside the colony limits. The sun is brilliant and high in the red sky as we head for the towering glass and metal building that houses the military complex.

. . .

The military complex is a strange place. First off, it's extremely intimidating due to its sheer size. Secondly, it's a strange mixture of Metal residence, tactical training facility, and prison. There's a lot of glass, steel, and concrete. Quite frankly the place gives me the creeps. The back of the facility houses the prison, which is beneath the building. The front of the building is the secure entrance that leads to both the military offices and the residences. Almost all Balanced Metals live inside this building. I suppose that says something about the number of Balanced versus Unbalanced. To the building's front is Pax Park. I shudder remembering how Li was taken over by the Imminent Darkness in that park. I'd rather not go back there.

"You'd better cloak yourself," Li says. "Because you're a wanted woman in more ways than one." I press the button on the underside of my wrist and Cerise lets out a little gasp as my body and everything on my person seemingly disappears into thin air. Really, it's an energy wave manipulation. But I was never one for science.

Cerise steps forward and jabs at the air, poking me hard in the ribs.

"Ow!"

"Ohmigosh, I'm so sorry! I didn't think you'd feel it."

"She's still here, just our eyes can no longer perceive it," Sloan explains wrapping an arm around my shoulder. "So the plan is we'll take this specimen inside and try to convince Michaela it's important to find out just what this insect is. That of course, most likely won't be easy. You guys really should stay here…"

"I refuse to go to that place," Li practically growls.

"No. No that's a horrible idea," I agree.

"What place? Could someone please tell me what's going on?" Cerise's eyes dart from Li to where my disembodied voice emanates.

"It's not important. I'll…show Cerise around."

I cock my head to the side. "Is that such a good idea?"

"We won't get into any trouble. I promise." A slight shimmer of his angular features.

I snort. "Yeah, I've heard that one before."

"No, that's actually a good idea," Sloan agrees and I wish he could see my withering glare right now. His hand squeezes my shoulder as if he doesn't need to see my face to know which expression I am wearing. "Cerise needs to know the layout of the colony. It's important for her safety in case we ever become separated." He glances at his watch. "Let's meet back here in an hour. Hopefully, that will be enough time."

"An hour. Aye, aye, Captain." Li salutes then grabs Cerise's hand, heading off in the direction of the rest of the Underground. Probably not the safest of places. But it's broad daylight and he's immortal, so I guess I don't have too much to worry about. Still, my stomach does a little flip flop in protest as they disappear down the sidewalk.

CHAPTER 26

The small glass entryway can lead one of two ways, one to a lobby with a bank of elevators and another with more security checks. The military side requires identification of various levels, however, it's a little more lax on the residential side depending on the security personnel working that day. Sloan breezes through and before I know it we're taking the elevator up to the fourth floor. There is no entrance to the first through third floors from this side of the building. In the privacy of the elevator Sloan reaches for my hand and places a gentle kiss on the back of my knuckles.

The elevators slide open and we step into the hallway which is all sleek floors and creepy silver sconces. All the doors are painted white and the apartment numbers are painted in black. We stop in front of a door marked 411 and he presses the bottom of the small intercom attached to the wall beside the door. A few seconds pass.

"Yes?" comes a voice, except it's not Michaela. I freeze for only a beat before I realize that it's Bina.

"It's me, Mom." Sloan replies. He looks down at me and grins.

The multiple locks tumble and the door slowly opens. Bina is standing in fuzzy purple slippers and a shabby bathrobe. Her gray hair is frizzy and sticking every which way, but her gray eyes are sharp and discerning. When she sees Sloan, she breaks into a toothless smile and pulls him in for a hug. The years and gift of the Sight have not always been kind to Bina. After releasing him she yanks me into her for an embrace. There's no hiding from the Sight.

She pulls us both in and shuts the door behind us. "Ye may as well uncloak yerself. Michaela's off at work." She waves a dismissive hand and heads into the apartment's small living room which contains one armchair, a small loveseat, and two barstools at the eat-in-kitchen's overhanging countertop. There's a large glass window opposite the kitchen, and Bina has the black curtains pulled wide as she stares at the tops of some trees pressed against the red sky.

I press the uncloak button.

"I see yeh saved him?" I forgot, now that I've gotten used to it, how obvious it is that Sloan's been drained of his Water. No pun intended. With a single glance, anyone can see that his scales are missing replaced with smooth, tanned skin.

"Yes." I say, but it comes out more of a whisper. She turns around and peers into Sloan's face. We're all still standing in the middle of the tiny living room. Her hand runs along his now-smooth right cheek.

"Still handsome," she chuckles then sits down in the armchair.

After the attempted MindCleanse, Bina was much weakened. Her recovery has progressed in leaps and bounds, but she still looks tired and there's no denying the fact that the events of the past month or so have aged her. She gestures for us to sit and we squeeze onto the small couch. "As much as I'd like to think it, I know ye didn't come just to visit yer old mum. So out with it."

A guilty look passes over Sloan's face, but he pulls out the test tube containing the insect. "We actually wanted to ask Michaela to run some tests on this." He hands the corked tube to Bina.

"We think the colony may be in danger."

"I see," she says as she inspects the contents inside the glass. Such a simple statement can have multiple meanings for someone like Bina. She uncorks the tube and sniffs, crinkling her nose before replacing the cork and handing it back to Sloan. "It smells of death."

I swallow the lump that's formed in my throat. I may like her and she may be Sloan's mom, but sometimes Bina frightens me. Just a little. Maybe a lot. "Whatever it is, it killed my friend Ahna. The one you met."

"Ah, yes. The girl with the long black hair."

"That's the one. She…disappeared for some time, at least according to her brother. And she was acting strange before we left. She was so angry. Mostly, at me." I glance down at my hands.

"Go on." Bina encourages, knowing that there's more to the story. She rests her head back on the chair and closes her eyes as if waiting for me to tell her a bedtime story.

"Well, the last time we were here the Imminent Darkness took over her twin, Li's, body and attacked me. We got away, but not before he was seriously injured."

"We used a memory ring to travel to the Land of Earth and to Novea. There she gave Li an elixir out of the Wood stone." Sloan taps his fingers on his leg, nervously waiting for Bina's response.

"Indeed. The Imminent Darkness is most unhappy about that. The balance is still not tipped in its favor. The boy was made immortal in order to save his life, I take it?"

"Yes, that's true. It was the only way to save him. And during our stay that's when Ahna started acting stranger. Once, Li was healed and my father brought them back home, he said she would disappear for long periods of time with no explanation. When I found her she looked as if all the life had been sucked out of her. Her hair was a wreck. She was dirty and there was dried blood on the corner of her mouth. And her eyes were wild. When she finally—" But my voice breaks off before I can finish.

"When she finally died, Ka said that a swarm of those…things…came up and out of her mouth and flew toward the colony. That one in there, in the tube, fell out of her ear. It was still alive, but died pretty quickly," Sloan finishes for me.

Bina's forehead furrows and her thin lips form a frown.

"And did your friend happen say anything before she died?"

I swallow again, my throat suddenly dry as the desert. "Only that I couldn't win because I wasn't strong enough. Except I know that she was lying."

One eye opens and peers at me.

"My new gift," I mumble. I haven't even told Sloan about it yet. "I can tell when people are lying. Their features shimmer, like I'm looking into a pool of cloudy water."

Sloan puts a hand on my leg and leans a shoulder into me. "Well, then I guess we're a bit more even. I can slip into your thoughts and you can tell if I'm being dishonest." He frowns. "Not that I've ever been…" A flush creeps up his neck and blossoms over his cheeks.

Bina ignores him and continues her train of thought. "So, the last time yeh was here was two weeks ago. Whatever was inside her incubated for at least that long."

"Two weeks?" I glance at Sloan. It seemed we were only gone for a few days. Of course, I knew that to be untrue.

"Assuming this guy's the same." She points at the tube in Sloan's hand. "Then that's how long we have to figure out what it is, create an antidote, and stop it because most likely, it's already started."

"But why would the Imminent Darkness want to ki—?" My words are cut off as the locks on the door tumble.

"Mom, I'm home! Did I hear you talking to someone?"

Michaela.

. . .

Hastily, I press the button on the inside of my wrist. There's the sound of something being dropped onto the floor then heavy footsteps. Michaela enters into the small living space, her long blonde hair in a perfect ponytail and the metallic threads glittering against her ivory skin. Her eyes have dark circles beneath them. She slips out of a black jacket with some kind of identification badge clipped to the front pocket and tosses it over one of the stools.

"Oh. It's you," she says to Sloan by way of greeting.

Michaela and I used to get along okay. When I first found out who Sloan really was and before she realized just how intricately I was tied into her brother's life. She moves to sit on the couch, right for my lap, but Sloan slides over offering her the space closer to Bina. She gives Sloan an odd look before sitting down. I've been squished into a sliver of the couch, and Sloan's left leg is resting on top of my right thigh.

"Why, hello, Sis. Good to see you too."

"Still alive, I see."

"Now, now, my children. Play nice," Bina scolds. "Yer home early."

"Actually, I'm not. I just came by to see how you were doing and to grab something to eat. They need me to work late." Michaela rests her head back on the couch and closes her eyes. She looks like she could fall asleep at the drop of a hat.

"Again?" Bina scowls.

Michaela opens one blue eye. "It would be a lot easier if Sloan's little girlfriend would just turn herself in. She's half of my problem. First, she's somehow involved with whatever happened in the Fire Building. Which is still being investigated. Then she was also involved with the prisoners from Council Hall, and on top of that she was spotted by one of the military personnel in Pax Park a couple of weeks ago before supposedly evaporating into thin air."

"One eighteen-year-old girl can't be guilty of all those things,"

Bina replies sensibly.

"Whose side are you on, Mother?"

"Nobody's. Just stating the obvious." Bina sucks on her bottom lip and takes an interest in the afghan she's spread across her lap.

"What's the other half of your problem?" Sloan asks. The test tube is back in the front pocket of his hoodie and I can see his hands fiddling with it.

"Those damn Imminent Darkness characters are running amuck, in case you haven't noticed. But you probably haven't because you're always disappearing with that fugitive girlfriend of yours."

I feel Sloan stiffen beside me.

"Firstly, you know nothing about Ka, Michaela. So don't act like you do. Secondly, I am well aware of the Imminent Darkness and what they do, where they go, and who they think they work for. But you don't even know the half of it. Soon you're going to have much bigger problems to deal with." Sloan's voice is icy as it slides from his lips.

I remember how when Michaela haughtily told him I'd be the death of him that he'd laughed at her words. They used to seem so close. When Sloan was just my teacher, I actually thought she was his girlfriend because she was always around. And I wasn't exactly thinking clearly due to the jealousy I was unknowingly experiencing. Now they seem so distant. Worlds apart. What happened? Am I solely to blame?

"What do you mean by that?" she snaps, sitting up at full attention. "How could *you* possibly know?"

Sloan slips the test tube out of his pocket. Instead of recoiling, Michaela looks somewhat interested. "Because I've seen things. While you're holed up in your office doing your military intelligence thing, I'm actually out there finding things. Not thinking in theories and making up lies."

"What is it?"

"We don't know. I was actually hoping, if you could set aside your pride for all of two seconds, that you would be able to find out." He hands her the tube and she moves it side-to-side so that the dead insect rolls around in the glass enclosure.

"Tell me again why I should care about some bug?"

"Because that bug crawled out of the ear of a girl who died. In a matter of days she went from healthy and vibrant to dead. It was as if all the life was sucked out of her." Sloan's voice catches at the word dead, but he swallows it down with a gulp.

"And you think this bug did that to her?" Michaela's face is skeptical.

"Yes. And I think that the bug is carrying some kind of sickness. That's what killed her. Not necessarily the bug itself."

"You think this bug contains, what, a plague or something?" She peers into the test tube as if her vision is microscopic.

"Yes."

"But this is only one bug."

"Before she died a swarm came out of her. It had been incubating inside of her. Someone had put it there. Witnesses say the swarm flew toward the colony. A lot of people could be in danger.

We don't know what it is. Nor do we know how to cure it."

"The labs have some antidotes from some of the Old Earth plagues. But this could possibly be different. At least it's something to start with while they analyze the insect's DNA. It's kind of ingenious actually, to use a human body as an incubator." Her eyes are unfocused as she stares at the tiny black dot, and I feel my insides curl in on themselves. It's not ingenious. It's sick.

Sloan's voice is stern. "That girl didn't deserve to die."

Michaela ignores him. "What about these so-called witnesses?"

"What about them?"

"Can I interview them? Where are they?" She glances up and blinks as if seeing the room for the very first time. Her brow furrows. "What happened to your face?"

Sloan runs a hand along the smooth skin of his right cheek. "There was an incident. But everything's fine."

Michaela's silent for a beat before her eyes narrow. "It was her. Wasn't it?"

"You wouldn't understand," Sloan says simply.

And he's right. She wouldn't. She wouldn't understand that it was the only choice we had to save his life. She wouldn't understand that he was going to be some sort of slave for a demented, ego-centric goddess. She wouldn't understand that a mermaid risked her life to save her brother's. Michaela only believes what she can see with her own two eyes and only believes what the evidence puts forth. She works in facts and figures, not worlds filled with immortal goddesses, mythical creatures, and ancient darkness.

"You're right. I wouldn't." Her voice is cold, but not as cold as the daggers that shoot from her eyes. She glances down and her head tilts, eyes narrowing in suspicion. "Is that her messenger bag?"

I cringe. My bag is sitting on the floor beside Sloan's feet. It's not on my person. Therefore, it's uncloaked.

Sloan shrugs. "I brought it with me."

Michaela leaps to her feet, still holding the corked test tube in her fist. "You brought her bag with you?" Her tone is accusatory.

"It's just a messenger bag. You know. It holds stuff."

"She's here, isn't she?" Her eyes dart around wildly. "She's hiding somewhere? Mother, what did you do with her?"

But Bina only shakes her head. I'm not completely sure how Bina's Sight works. I think some of it comes to her in dreams, and other times I know she needs to be touching the person or holding onto something that belongs to them. Her face gives no indication that she knew this would happen.

Michaela has begun lifting up the couch cushions, like I somehow shrank and am hiding beneath them. Which I guess isn't too far from the truth. She abandons that when she reaches Sloan's side of the couch, instead marching down the hall and banging bedroom doors as she flings them open. No doubt searching for me in closets and beneath the beds. Bina glances in the direction of the front door. I get up as quickly as I can, take two steps and plow right into Michaela as she's headed back toward the kitchen.

"Ow! What the heck?" she yelps, stumbling backward and rubbing her nose which had just plowed into my shoulder. I could run. But Michaela is too quick, she reaches for the air, making contact with my arm and digs her fingernails in. I wince in pain, but no one can see it.

Sloan must realize what's going on because he leaps to his feet and takes a step toward Michaela. "Stop it!"

"I don't know what kind of tricks you two are getting at," she says, eyes darting between Sloan and Bina, who is now also standing. "But this girl is wanted by the Xon 9 military. And for good reason. She's obviously part of this Imminent Darkness."

"Don't be ridiculous," Bina scolds, placing her hands on her hips. She's a full head shorter than Michaela, but her eyes look like razors ready to cut her down to size.

"Ridiculous? You two are the ridiculous ones! With your nonsensical visions and harboring a known fugitive of the law. She has information that can protect the safety of the entire colony. And if she is guilty of her crimes, then she needs to pay the consequences."

Sloan glances at the test tube. "I don't think that whatever knowledge you assume Ka knows is going to help ensure the safety of the colony."

Michaela follows his glance. "Maybe she's the one who did it. Infected the girl you were talking about." Somehow her thumb finds the button on my cloaking cuff and I return to being in full view.

I scowl at her. "She was my best friend."

"Most criminals eventually sink to the unthinkable," she snarls. Her eyes are rabid as she clutches the test tube in one fist and my wrist in the other. Her ponytail has pieces falling out. "Hand me my identification badge."

Nobody moves.

"Damn it. Hand me my badge before I press charges against both of you for harboring a criminal and a fugitive." Her face appears clear, her angular cheekbones jutted in a smirk. No lies.

Sloan's face falls as he stares in shock at his sister. "Michaela. Really?"

"I told you she would be the death of you." Irritated, Michaela uses her thumb to pull something out of her pocket. Handcuffs. She snaps them over my wrists.

"Yeh can't be serious," Bina says softly. She reaches for the jacket and unsnaps the badge and hands it to her daughter. "Isn't this a little much?"

"The colony deserves answers."

"Surely, there's another way to get them," Bina says, hands out, palms up. My mind is reeling. Michaela has no idea what I'm capable of, doesn't know that I could burn her or tie her up in green vines with a single thought. My eyes meet Sloan's. He gives an almost imperceptible shake of his head. I swallow.

"Personally, I like to go right to the source. Did I mention that there's a nice bounty on her head as well? I've been wanting to upgrade the apartment." She smiles and it's all icy, white teeth.

"A bigger apartment is more important than yer own kin?" Bina asks, crossing her arms. Sloan said Michaela was always the odd one out. That Bina, Finn, and he were the gifted ones and that Michaela always had to work hard at everything. Yet, she took care of Bina after she almost died, having her move into the small apartment. And I know in her own warped way, that her hatred for me is out of protection for her big brother.

Michaela begins dragging me to the door. I want to cry or kick or scream, but I'm surrounded in some kind of emotional abyss. We reach the door and Michaela turns, one arm looped through mine and the other holding the test tube.

"No. But the safety of thousands of people is more important to me than only two." She holds her chin up high as she shoves me out the door. In the hallway I turn back and see Bina put a reassuring hand on Sloan's arm. His face is contorted with both hurt and anger.

Michaela doesn't bother to shut the door as she shoves me along toward the elevators. Down the hallway I hear Bina's voice drift after us.

"Tell that to yer father."

CHAPTER 27

There's no point in putting up a fight. I'm not going to harm Michaela and give her even more reason to hate my guts. As if, in her mind, she doesn't have enough reason already. She drags me roughly to the bank of elevators and uses a fist to hit the down button.

"I'd be careful with that," I say nodding at the test tube clenched in her hand.

"I don't need advice from a criminal," Michaela snarls as she yanks me into the elevator.

The doors slide silently closed. We sail down past the ground floor and Michaela pulls me down an unfamiliar corridor. The fluorescent lights are jarring. Everything is white. The floors. The walls. There are no windows. We pass no doors. At the end of the hallway is a double set of steel doors with a sleek black box to the right.

Michaela scans her identification badge and the doors swing open. More bright lights and starkness. There's a sleek white counter and behind it sits a man in all black. His appearance is foreboding contrasted against the whiteness around him, like a black smudge on an otherwise pristine palette. He glowers at me and then glowers at Michaela. Apparently this guy is in a bad mood, criminal or not. His dark, bushy eyebrows glance down at the computer in front of him. And then he taps his fingers impatiently on the counter top.

"Braden, M.I." Michaela says thrusting me forward so that the edge of the counter top squishes into my gut. She waves her identification badge in front of the man's face. He rolls his eyes.

"You military intelligence types are all the same. I knew about you before you even got off the elevator. All cameras scanned you and your…apprehension. I know you're Michaela Braden, aged twenty-four, with the military for three years, your brother is a Water and a teacher, your mother is a Metal who works in the Black Bazaar, and your father is in prison." He smirks as if he finds the last bit amusing. "If you farted, I'd know about it. But you…" He glances at me and the cocky smile fades ever so slightly. "I don't seem to have as much information. Ka Waylon. Seventeen, a new Fire. Mother is an Earth researcher, father a Wood, liege to the Council."

"Eighteen," I correct, even though I don't know why. It seems so trivial with everything else that's been going on.

Michaela glares at the man, who on second glance isn't much older than she is. "I'd like to get my apprehension processed for questioning."

He raises an eyebrow. "What's she guilty of? Breaking curfew?" he asks sarcastically.

"Hardly. Maybe if you worked in intelligence instead of doing a monkey's work in processing, you'd know that she's a wanted fugitive for both treason and evading arrest."

The man's face glowers. He types something into the computer then gives Michaela a hard stare, his blue eyes anything but friendly. He pushes a button. "Mack Eighty-Four, we have an apprehension. Request transport to a holding cell until questioning."

Michaela raises an eyebrow as if to say *I told you so*, but the man just returns to his computer and begins typing like we aren't even here. I'm tempted to tell Michaela that she'd have a lot more friends if she'd just try to be a little more pleasant, but I bite my tongue.

The sound of heavy footsteps can be heard coming down the single hallway to the left of the counter. It turns out Mack is a woman. She's a bit round about the middle, but looks like she could crush your hand in her handshake. Her blonde hair is cropped short in a spiky style and she's wearing scarlet red lipstick. Her eyes are sharp and discerning. She is not at all what I expected.

"Where's the apprehension?" she asks looking around the lobby.

"Here," I say before Michaela or Sir Grumpy Pants can speak for me.

"You?" she asks casting a doubtful glance at the man behind the counter. But he just shrugs and rolls his eyes toward Michaela.

Michaela shoves me forward. Then, satisfied that I'm in hands that won't let me escape, and without sparing me a parting glance, she heads back toward the door, the test tube still clenched in her fist. I can only hope that she gets the tests run as soon as possible and that they can make a vaccine. Because if they can't, I'm afraid to think of how many people will suffer the same fate as Ahna.

Mack clears her throat and wraps her sausage fingers around my forearm. A tattoo of a skull with worms crawling out its eyeholes moves along the brawny muscles of her forearm. I gulp.

She guides me back toward the hallway she'd appeared from only minutes before.

"This way."

. . .

We enter through a second set of steel doors. Everything is white and it's disorienting. The only sound is the heavy plod of Mack's boots. We reach yet another set of steel doors, this time there's a keypad to the left and another door to the right.

Mack presses a code into the keypad and the door slides open.

"Step inside there. You'll find a folded-up jumpsuit and some shoes on the floor inside a bag. Leave all your belongings inside that bag." She unlocks the cuffs and nudges me toward the doorway.

I peer into the room and take a tentative step. This all seems to be spiraling out of control. Sloan told me not to use my powers, but would he rather me be here? Being treated like a criminal even though I've done nothing wrong.

Or have I?

Maybe wanting things to change is a crime.

I step into the room and a light automatically turns on. The door slides shut behind me and I hear the locking mechanism catch. This room is also entirely white. I guess they have a theme going on. There's no windows or other doors. One way in, one way out. I crouch near the bag that already has my name on it: Ka Waylon. I pull out the starched jumpsuit and sigh as I kick off my boots and begin to undress.

Why did Bina and Sloan not want to stop this? What am I supposed to learn? Besides the fact that Michaela cares more about her own agenda than about her family. What did Bina mean when she said, *Tell that to yer father.* ?

I fold up my clothes and stuff them back into the bag. The so-called shoes are more like cloth slippers. The light catches my wrist and I remember that I'm still wearing the cloaking cuff. I slip it off and then unzip the front of the uniform and drop the cuff into my underwear. Not like these things come with pockets. And, unlike Cerise, my hair is too short to store odds and ends. I re-zip my uniform, the fabric thick and rough against skin.

Mack didn't give me further instructions so I'm about to knock on the door to let her know I'm done when a brilliant blue light engulfs the room. A robotic voice emanates from an unknown source.

"Ka Waylon. Fire. Prison Identification Number 8392. Charges: Arson, Treason, Fleeing Arrest. Status: Holding until interrogation is complete. Threat Level: Four." The voice repeats all of this a second time, I suppose in case you didn't catch it the first time. Treason? Threat level four? How many threat levels are there? Is a four good or bad? I suppose all levels are bad depending on whose side you're on.

After the voice is done the blue light changes back to white. There's a click and something lowers from the ceiling. Some kind of strange metal device with hinges. And claws. Before I can run or move, it snaps around my wrists holding them above my head. I feel an uncomfortable snap in my shoulder blade. There's a buzzing sound and another hinge pops out of the metal arm holding my left wrist. The buzzing sounds oddly familiar. Like the buzz of a tattoo needle. That's when I realize it sounds like a tattoo needle because that's exactly what it is.

The buzzing needle finds my trapped right wrist and I feel the burning, scratching sensation as it deposits ink into the top layer of my epidermis. Then almost as quickly as it started the buzzing stops. The claw holding the tattoo needle disappears back inside the metal arm. Both pinchers release my wrists and the two metal arms fold into the larger singular metal body before disappearing back into the ceiling.

I rub my wrist, smearing a little bit of blood. 8392 is inked onto the inside of my right wrist. The automated voice announces that processing is complete. The steel door slides back open. Mack waits outside twirling the handcuffs around her finger with a bored expression on her face. When I exit and the door slides closed behind me, she roughly pulls my arms behind my back and snaps the cuffs back on. Deciding that I must not be much of a threat, she puts a hand on my shoulder and guides me down the hallway to the other door.

Despite the uniform and my new prisoner identification number, I don't feel like a criminal. Probably because I'm not. Mack puts in another key code and the next door slides open. This hallway is much different than the first.

There are windows along the right side of the wall. Each window reveals a room with a person in a jumpsuit that matches mine. There's a small bed and a toilet, but that's it. I turn my head as we pass someone using the toilet.

"They're one-sided. We can see in, but they can't see out," Mack informs me.

In the next window the prisoner is curled up in the fetal position on the bed. Someone else is pacing. The last window reveals a woman with hair curled behind her ears rocking back and forth in the corner, her knees pressed against her chest. My heart begins to pound against my ribcage as we round a corner.

"What is this place?" I ask.

Mack bypasses the obvious and answers. "Level three threats."

If these are the level three threats, I'm afraid to ask where the level four threats are kept.

"I thought I was just going into a holding cell." We pass more windows, but I turn my head so that I'm facing the white wall opposite instead.

"That would be the case. If you were a level one. But apparently, someone thinks otherwise."

My first thought is Michaela. She could never begin to

understand. Everything is so black and white to her despite the eccentricities of her family. We reach an elevator. Mack inserts her badge into a device on the wall and the elevator silently slides open. We step in. Every surface is mirrored and there's a camera in the corner.

My short ponytail has slipped out and my face is thinner and more angular than the last time I looked. We begin to move, but the ride is quickly over. The elevator comes to a stop and we step out into a hallway that seems to be lined with stainless steel. But instead of windows lining the wall, there are doors, only revealed by the large rivets that line each doorframe. Each door has a plaque next to it with a number. I can hear someone pounding and yelling behind one of the doors. But the sound is disorienting. It echoes off the steel walls and reverberates between the steel floor and ceiling. The result is the sound seems to hum well after it's stopped.

Mack stops at a door. The number on the plaque matches the number now forever tattooed on my right wrist. Does Michaela realize what she's done? The one hope that can stop the Imminent Darkness and I'm about to be trapped in a room coated in stainless steel. Naively, she doesn't realize that she's giving the Imminent Darkness exactly what it wants. Things will only get worse. Chaos will ensue and in its wake, death. And I'm powerless to stop it because Bina and Sloan obviously wanted this to happen. It could have been a vision. Or maybe it was in that damned book that I refused to read. If I had read it then maybe I would have known. I could have prepared myself.

Because, if I'm being honest, I'm afraid. The hair on the back of my neck prickles as another scream reverberates down the hallway, seemingly coming from all directions. Fear is a circular emotion. It feeds on itself to grow stronger. It has the capacity to cripple even the strongest man to inaction. But it also has the power to spur even the weakest man to action. Fear works in the primitive part of the brain all the way back to hunter-gather times. It is the idea to flee and hide, or to stay and fight. Every ounce of me wants to flee. To use my powers to escape this labyrinth of prison cells and go back to the tent city. But there's a higher power at work here. There always has been. I thought that I was in control, but I was wrong. I'm as much of a pawn as anyone else. Someone else is always moving the pieces and setting the plays into motion. I can't let my fear ruin me like that woman in the level three, rocking back and forth in the corner. Or I can use my fear to my advantage. I can use the dilation of my pupils and the heightened sense of hearing that comes when fear causes the adrenaline to course through my veins so I can more easily see the unseen and hear the words that aren't being said.

Mack presses a code into the key pad that is embedded into the steel wall. The lock tumbles, sending an echo across the hallway. She pulls the heavy door open using two hands. Then gestures.

"Home sweet home, Doll."

I am not prepared. But I have no choice. There is something here for me. Waiting. I have a mission. This is bigger than me. The steel door slides closed with a reverberating thud, locking me in.

I am afraid.

ABOUT THE AUTHOR

Jennifer L. Kelly is a middle childhood educator. She resides in Cleveland, Ohio. When she isn't writing, she can be found fangirling over *Doctor Who*, doing yoga, spending time with her dog, taking photos for her #bookstagram, or making candles for her Etsy shop: TheBookishFlame. This is her second series for young adults. Her first novel, *The Prophecy: The Lucia Chronicles Book 1,* was published in January 2014. Visit her website **Skim.Scheme.Scribble: www.jenniferlkelly.com** Or say *HI!* :

info@jenniferlkelly.com

JenniferLKelly3

AuthorJenniferLKelly

AuthorJenniferLKelly

ACKNOWLEDGEMENTS

Somehow I have made it through four books in this series. Writing a series is much different than writing a trilogy. Not only with characters and plot lines, but with people who are willing to invest for the long haul. Firstly, I'd like to thank my Dad. He's told me numerous times that I am just as good as "those other YA authors" whose books he's read. Thank you for believing in me. I'd also like to thank my Advanced Readers because I know what a commitment I asked for when I said I was releasing five books in twelve months. For those who've made it this far, I love you and thank you! I also cannot forget to send thanks to the amazing Rebecca Solow who created my map of Xon 9 and the Elemental Abyss, and to the talented Joshua Jadon for my Elemental Star. I may have to ask Zora to ink me soon. Lastly, thank you to the rest of my friends and family, as well as my bookish friends on #bookstagram!

Turn the page for the beginning of ...

SECRET OF METAL

The Elementals Book 5

09.12.17

It wasn't supposed to be this way. Li was never supposed to get hurt. He was never supposed to be drained of his Fire. My mom and dad should both still be here. But they're not. And Ahna. Ahna wasn't supposed to die. But she did.

If I was feeling exceptionally sorry for myself, I'd say that it was all my fault. Maybe it is. But in my heart I know that it isn't. My mom always said, "Head or heart, Kata?" Well, I said heart. And my heart says none of this is my fault. It's the fault of the Imminent Darkness.

What's the Imminent Darkness you ask? It's an ancient, evil force that seeks to restore balance to the Universe. The ID's MO is deception, torture, and murder. A long time ago five sisters— goddesses of the Universe—were tricked by an old codger, the Imminent Darkness in disguise. Long story short, he created rivalry between the sisters and each one was given a stone. An Elemental stone. Because the sisters could no longer get along, their parents Raj and Katayun—King and Queen of the Universe respectively, and also my grandparents—created a land for each of the daughter to inhabit. One each for Earth, Water, Wood, Fire, and Metal. My mother, Novea, ruled the Land of Earth. Eventually, she came to live on Xon 9 and fell in love with a mortal man, my dad, Absalom. One thing led to another as these things tend to do, and they had me. Thing is, there's no one else like me in the world. My mother's sisters gifted me with the Elemental stones upon my birth, and in so doing a part of each Element. But that was a very dangerous thing to do. Soon, I was showing aptitude at a young age for each Element. Which naturally, just wouldn't do because here on Xon 9 you get to choose one and only one Element.

So what's a mother to do? She consulted an old Metal woman with the Sight. The Seer kept the stones safe for a while, but eventually she gave them back to my mother to throw into the Elemental Abyss. It was an act to protect me. Only, it has had the complete opposite effect. Because eventually I found out who—or what—I truly am. I am the Impossible Girl. I am all possibilities and yet I am none.

The Imminent Darkness is taking over my planet. It has hurt many people that I love. It killed my best friend. And its human minions have terrorized the colonists of Xon 9. Power is the reward. Fear is the currency. But no more. I will retrieve the Elemental stones and restore what's rightfully mine. I feel the pulse of Earth in my veins. The electricity of Fire in my blood. I have gained the wisdom of Wood, more than any normal teenager should have to bear when she should be thinking about boys and University, instead of saving the world. The gentle ferocity of Water fuels my spirit. Five stones. Four retrieved and destroyed. One left to go.

CHAPTER 1

I kick at the wall again. Pushing my soft-padded shoes against the steel wall. The bed is stiff and feels like plywood. The aches in my back subsided long ago. An agonizing scream echoes off the metal walls of the hallway. I close my eyes and listen to the pad of boots trotting down the hallway. Being here, in this cell, my senses all seem heightened.

The room is stark. Everything is stainless steel. The walls, the door, the ceiling, the toilet. Everything but the bed. When I close my eyes, I can hear the self-assured step of the Metal soldiers as they walk around. They're trained to run and barely make a sound, but if I close my eyes and the whiteness fills my head, then I can hear them. I've even come to identify some of their steps. The heavy-footed stride of the red-haired soldier. The toe-to-heal stride of the blonde with a penchant for sharp objects. The soft-scraping of the sound of

Michaela's boots.

She doesn't know that I know. But even in the dark, I can see. Her blonde hair, stripped of its luster. The chapped bottom lip from biting it so often over whether or not she did the right thing. She's sure she did the right thing. I can hear her as she presses her palm flush against the door and presses her forehead against its coolness. The slight rattle of her breath. Because she doesn't know what I already know. That it's only a matter of time before the entire colony is infected. Before what killed my best friend, kills them too. But I'm safe here in my little metal cocoon. Safe from the world outside. Micahela doesn't care that she betrayed me. But she does care that she betrayed her brother. She lifts her forehead from the door and I can almost see the resolution in those steely blue eyes, her hand curling into a fist.

She had no choice. I was a threat to the Leadership Council. It had to be done. The image of an old, now blind man drifts into her mind, like cobwebs long-forgotten in the corners of her mind. Did he deserve his punishment for speaking out against the Leadership Council? She shakes her head as if the cobwebs could fall out of her ears and onto the steel floor, where she grinds them beneath the heal of her black, military-issued combat boots. She was trained to uphold the law. But is the law always so black and white?

The glare of the light reflects off the web of silvery, metallic threads that line the right side of her face. She sighs softly. Again, the faintest of rattles. And I hear the soft scrap of her boots as she continues down the hallway, resigned to live with the choices she's made.

There's no sense of time in a cell with no windows. I lost track of the days long ago. I know I'm awake more than I sleep. My eyes feel as if they're full of sand. My almost shoulder length brown hair is knotted and greasy. I don't eat the food they give me. Well, besides the rock-hard bread. They can keep their mystery meat and so-called vegetable melody. More like vegetable catastrophe. I've lost weight. If I run my fingers over my jumpsuit and over my waist, I can count my ribs individually. What would Sloan say if he saw me now? I kick at the wall again. It makes a soft, muffled sound.

My chest feels constricted whenever I think about Sloan, as if my heart is trying to claw its way out and up my throat. Tears no longer sting the backs of my eyes when I think of him. I know it hasn't been that long, but has it been long enough? Those sea-green eyes and shaggy brown hair, beautiful silvery-green scales that used to line the side of his face, like the sea come to life. That's my Sloan. Assuming he's still mine. He is. My heart knows it. My head hopes it. But he hasn't visited me in my dreams. Neither has his mom, Bina.

The worst part of being in here is the not-doing. The Imminent Darkness is out there, creeping through the Elemental Abyss, its darkness seeping into the nooks and crannies of my home. The only home I've ever known. And I'm locked in here for no crime, except doing what I know is right and asking the questions no one wants to ask. The Imminent Darkness is feeding on the energy of the inhabitants of Xon 9, growing stronger as it devours their souls. And there's not a damn thing I can do about it.

There's a loud click. The sound of the keypad being accessed to open my cell. The door slides open and a tall, red-haired guy with a neck as big as my waist enters. The door slides closed behind him. He wears all black and has a gun holstered on his belt. His uniform is meticulous. The garish lighting causes the right side of his face to appear in a soft blur of silver. It's the heavy-footed soldier arrived with my dinner—or breakfast—one can never tell.

"Dinner, Number 8392." He sets the tray at the foot of the bed and takes a step back. I slide myself upright and swing my legs around so they're no longer against the wall. I don't answer. I never answer.

Officer Red Hair doesn't appear much older than me. I'm eighteen and I peg him for maybe Sloan's age, twenty-two. Most likely he's only been in this position for a couple of moons. He crosses his arms and cuts me a glare, hazel eyes narrowed.

"Are you planning on starving yourself to death?"

"It would be quicker," I reply before I can stop myself, my voice rusty from disuse.

His mouth quirks up in a grin. "Oh, she speaks. Here, I thought you were a mute."

I narrow my eyes at him and give him my best condescending smile. Unfortunately, I'm quite out of practice.

He glances at the tray. "I wouldn't eat the meat if I were you, but the noodles aren't so bad." He nods and for the first time I notice the greenish glob of what could possibly pass as noodles made of seaweed on the tray. That is, if Xon 9 had surface water. I try not to gag. My face must turn a visible shade of green. "Like I said, you might want to try them. It would be an improvement from your regular rock-hard bread roll. Change it up a bit. Live a little."

I snort in reply. "Hard to live it up in a cell made of metal."

"Well, you never know." he says, shrugging. "I'll be back in a bit to collect the tray. Bon appetite, Princess."

I start at his words, but he's already turned his back to me as the door slides open and he steps back into the hallway. Princess. Only a handful of people have ever called me princess. Only two knew what I really am. Who my mother really is. One is dead. The other is Li. My heart begins to pound in my chest as if it will bust out of the jail that is my ribcage. I look around my cell. There are no cameras in the cells. There are cameras in the hallway, but none in the cells. I inch closer to the tray. The smell makes my stomach wretch. If not for the Imminent Darkness, the Leadership Council should be put to tribunal for making anyone eat this garbage, prisoner or not.

I swallow the urge to vomit and inch my fingers toward the tray. They don't give us utensils, just the tray and a small napkin. I pick up the roll and take a bite, practically cracking a tooth. As I chew I glare at the green glob. But he called me Princess. *Live a little. You never know.* I stop chewing and close my eyes. I take a deep breath. I can smell the staleness of the bread and the sea-like smell of the strange noodles. Wait. There it is. Just the hint of something metallic. That's the downside to taking away one of someone's senses, staring at metal walls all day, the other sense become heightened. Like superpowers. I don't need my Elemental gifts to confirm what my own nose has already told me.

I jab my fingers into the cold, gloop. The noodles are slippery, but it only takes me a second to find it. A thin, silver pen-like object. No cameras. I pull it out of the glob. There's a small, black button that slides along the side. My fingers find the small engraved marking before my eyes do, the letter X and the number 9 along with three interlocking circles. The sun and twin moons. On the opposite side is another engraving: a tiny symbol like an upside down Y. This is a military grade laser cutter. That can cut through anything. Like a steel door. *Princess.*

Li.

What can I say? I know a guy.

SECRET OF METAL

The Elementals Book 5

09.12.17

www.ingramcontent.com/pod-product-compliance
Lightning Source LLC
Chambersburg PA
CBHW022147170626
46807CB00005B/2104